ℱAIREST

An Unfortunate Fairy Tale
Book 2

Chanda Hahn

ISBN-13: 978-1478215776
ISBN-10: 1478215771
FAIREST
Copyright © 2012 by Chanda Hahn
Cover model Laurel Seawell
Cover design by Steve Hahn
Revised 6/1/13
This is a work of fiction. Names, characters, places and incidents are either the product of the author's imagination or are used fictitiously, and any resemblance to actual persons, living or dead, business establishments, events or locales is entirely coincidental.

www.chandahahn.com

Mirror, mirror on the wall
Who is the fairest of them all?

CHAPTER 1

Being ripped to pieces by Fae wasn't how she'd envisioned dying. Her lungs burned with the lack of oxygen, and a painful stitch stabbed her side. Mina gasped, gritted her teeth, and pumped her legs harder, trying to put even more distance between her and her pursuers. She turned a corner and took a chance to glance over her shoulder at the three very large Fae bearing down on her. They were quicker than she thought, and they were closing the distance fast. She was in serious trouble.

She knew this area of town, and saw that they were almost to the Tulleyway Bridge. Within seconds, she reached the steel fence with its glaring metal sign that read "No Trespassing." Sliding to her knees, Mina squeezed through a gap in the fence, scraping her arms in the process. As she looked over her shoulder, she saw her pursuers reach the fence and choose to scale it instead of squeezing through the impossibly small opening.

"Oh, crud," Mina blurted out, sprinting down the stairs leading to the underpass. The whole area was littered with trash, broken-down boxes, and old oil barrels that vagrants used on bitterly cold nights. The underpass was deserted. She wasn't sure what had possessed her to run here. Maybe it was fate.

A few days ago, Mina had felt something akin to a giant metaphysical shove that literally pushed her to the front door of The End Zone, sports bar and grill, and not even close to one of her normal venues. She'd heard about the famous eatery because it was co-owned by three former Chicago Bears football players. She fought the urge to enter the restaurant, but after three days of intense headaches, tingling feelings, and all of the shoves she kept getting in its direction, she finally gave in to the prompting. Mina knew that within the four walls of the restaurant, she would come face to face with her next quest.

She sat at a small side table, ordered a Coke and a basket of fries, and abruptly sent them back because they were still frozen in the middle and the soda was flat. After ten minutes in a very annoying wobbly chair, Mina got up and switched seats, twice. All three of the retired players witnessed Mina's actions, each from a different place in the room. Their reactions ranged from mild disgust to intense hatred.

When the last customer left, one of the men went to the door and flipped the sign to "Closed," restricting the occupancy down to four: Mina and the three Chicago Bears. The men barely tolerated looking at her. It wasn't until Mina, in an attempt to make small talk, made a comment about the Bears current win-loss status, and realized they weren't in the mood for a discussion and never would be.

Brown, the largest Bears player, leaned across Mina's table to sniff her hair. Her muscles tensed up, and she swallowed the last bite of her fry. She was petrified.

Brown exhaled loudly, stormed over to his colleagues, and growled out one word:

"Grimm."

Six hate-filled eyes looked her way.

Not needing any prodding, she jumped from her seat and ran out the door, barely beating the smallest bear by seconds. She looked over her shoulder and could see that he had transformed partway when he started to chase after her. He slammed into the closed glass door, shattering it into a thousand shimmering pieces. It slowed him down just enough for her to escape. It also confirmed her suspicion. They were Fae.

The bears regrouped and decided whether or not to chase her down, which gave her a thirty-second head start. She prayed that they would decide to let her live and not follow her, but it was obvious that her prayer wasn't about to be answered today.

She jumped around the garbage that littered the underpass while trying to pull the Grimoire out of her denim jacket. She would have to think on her feet if she wanted to outsmart three actual Chicago Fae Bears. In a random and wild thought, she briefly wondered if they'd helped or hindered the team during their professional careers.

Armed with only a magical notebook that could morph its shape and imprison Fae within its pages, she took in her surroundings and her enemy and devised a somewhat ludicrous, though foolproof plan.

In the last month, Mina had bonded more with the Grimoire, gaining confidence in its abilities, and trusting it to aid her, even to the point of completing three minor quests. It in no way made her as talented as her father, but it gave her self-confidence. However, tackling small fiendish ravens and troubling foxes was nothing compared to entrapping larger-than-life bears strong enough to rip off her head.

A roar behind her made her turn in surprise. Two of them were no longer hiding their Fae forms and had shifted fully. Their leader was older, with tufts of grey sprouting along his shoulder blades, giving him an otherworldly appearance. Their football jerseys ripped as they could no longer contain the bulk of their true Fae form.

Unprepared for the quick change, she bumped into an overturned barrel and fell down, skinning her knee. She shouldn't have looked back. Jumping to her feet, she saw the third bear coming down the spillway from the other direction. They had surrounded her. She hadn't counted on that.

"So, um, how do you like my trap?" Mina announced innocently, feeling skittish and nervous.

"Trap? I think it is you who are trapped, little Grimm," the smallest bear growled at her while stepping closer. His golden brown fur was littered with the broken glass of the shattered restaurant door.

"Who sent you after us?" the leader called out from behind her as he caught up to them. He was older, bigger, and slower. "Did the Fates tell you where we were? We were getting too powerful for their liking, weren't we? They don't like how we run our business over here. Well, that's just it — it's our business, not theirs."

"What does it matter if we eat a few humans every once in a while? We still pay our tithe to the courts. We still obey and appear when summoned. Who did we tick off to get you knocking at our door?" the largest one, Brown, demanded.

She felt disgusted, sick to her stomach at what she'd just heard. Had they just confessed to eating humans? Mina looked around under the bridge at the empty boxes and sleeping bags and realized where they found their food. This whole time, she thought she was leading them on a chase, but instead they were herding her…to their hunting grounds. She swallowed and felt her stomach drop.

"The Story," Mina answered, unsure of what else to say. "The Story sent me after you, or should I say, sent you to me."

"Story? We don't want any part of that." Brown walked closer to Mina. He flexed his shoulders and opened his hands to show her his large black claws. "We just want to conduct

4

our business our way. What say we let you live, and you take that cursed book and never come back?"

"Sorry, guys," Mina answered, trying to sound brave while her hands shook with fear. "That's just not gonna cut it. I can't let you continue with what you're doing. Story or no Story, you have to be stopped."

The smallest bear leaned forward, saliva dripping from his teeth in anticipation as he sauntered toward her. His voice came out muffled and slurred, his bear mouth unable to form clear precise words, which was proof that the youngest spent more time in human form. "Then we will just have to take care of you ourselves."

She looked up, and all three of them began to charge her. She grabbed the notebook and flung it open, concentrating as three giant gold bear traps sprouted from the ground. Each of the bears stopped in their tracks and began screaming in pain as, one by one, they were caught in a magical golden trap. The traps surrounded their ankles and anchored them to the ground, immobile.

Mina smiled in relief when it worked, but only for a moment, as the closest bear could still reach her with his long powerful paw. She looked up just in time to see him swipe for her head. She screamed and opened the Grimoire. A pure bright light shot out of the book, making the bears shrink back in fear. She held onto the Grimoire in desperation as the book grew hot and the Fae bears continued to fight against the magical traps while trying to dodge the light pouring from the book. Just like before, a powerful wind picked up, lifting them into the air and pulling them into its pages.

They came closer, and Mina dropped the book to the ground and moved away, scared of getting pulled into the book as well. She hid her eyes from the light and waited until the rushing wind stopped. When all was quiet, she looked around and saw that once again the book was closed. Slowly, she stood, dusted off her dirty and ripped jeans, and picked up the book to check on its contents.

What once was a blank page was now filled with a beautiful illustration — a perfect likeness of her attackers in their true Fae forms. To the side of the three bears was the silhouette of a young girl who looked like Mina. She flipped to the beginning and saw words scrawled across the index. She had finished another quest, and this one without help!

CHAPTER 2

"Earth to Mina! Yoo-hoo!"

"Hmm?" Mina lifted her head from its perch on the stack of books splayed across her school desk to gape at Nan.

She hadn't heard a word her best friend had spoken in the last few minutes because she'd been staring out the school window toward the aquatics building. Any minute now *he* would be walking out of that particular grey building with the rest of his water polo team. She was wishing — hoping — no, praying for a chance to catch a glimpse of him. Every day it was the same: She would wait here, stare out the window, watch him walk by, and hope he would turn in her direction and smile at her the way he used to. Well, not every day, just each day she had detention. And because of the narrow-minded, unforgiving Mrs. Porter, she had detention again today.

Nan spoke again.

"I'm sorry. What did you say?" Mina asked lamely, resting her head on her hand. She'd been too exhausted from her Grimm tasks and her hopeless crush on Brody to be an attentive friend lately.

"I don't understand what has come over you these last few weeks. You're mentally preoccupied, you're never home, and you've been really secretive. If I didn't know better, I would think you're seeing someone. Hey, now that I think about it, you have been avoiding that new kid, Jared, like the plague." Nan squealed in delight, her golden hair bouncing with each head bob. "It's him, isn't it?"

Nan looked striking today in her cute skinny jeans, trendy boat shoes, sparkly blue nails, light blue band T-shirt, and fedora hat. She was simply the loveliest girl in school and only had detention because of her insane habit of constantly using her phone in class. She slid into the desk opposite Mina and leaned over, cutting off Mina's view of outside.

Mina frowned and leaned farther out of her chair. Nan mimicked her movement and leaned with her. When Mina didn't respond, Nan reached over and playfully tugged on Mina's brown hair.

"Ouch, Nan!" Mina grumbled, and swatted at her friend's hand.

"Nan, what? Tell me what's going through that square noggin of yours."

"My head is not square."

"No, but you sure are becoming one. You used to be a lot more fun. Tell me, is it Charlie?" Nan crossed her legs and arms, trying to hide her worry. Her foot wiggled back and forth nervously.

"No, it's not Charlie. He's fine."

Nan sighed in relief but then quickly asked, "Is it Sara?"

"No, Nan, it's not my mom!" Mina leaned back into her chair in a moment of frustration.

"Well, then, what is it? I give up. I will give you my favorite CD. No, wait, my favorite pair of shoes if you tell me. No, wait. I'll let you *borrow* my favorite pair of shoes." Nan gave her an unconvincing smile.

Mina didn't hear the rest of Nan's attempt at bartering because the person she'd been waiting for appeared. Brody Carmichael rounded the corner with his gym bag slung over his shoulder. Mina's breath caught in her throat and she forgot everything, even where she was.

There he was: perfection. Tan skin, square jaw, blue twinkling eyes, and blond hair that curled slightly since it was still wet from the pool. Brody threw his head back and laughed at something his friend T.J. said.

Mina's heart began to break all over again. Someone called out to the boys, and they turned expectantly and waited.

A girl of equal perfection, in a cheerleader uniform, ran up to greet them. Her naturally curled ponytail swayed from side to side, and Mina had the distinct urge to take a pair of scissors to the offending blonde plait. Mina had no choice but to watch the exchange between them with narrowed eyes. It was obvious by the way Brody's mouth turned down that he was beginning to lose patience with the girl. Mina wanted to scream encouragement through the glass and across the courtyard toward Brody. Apparently, the conversation was over, because Savannah White flounced away smiling like a Cheshire cat. Brody's shoulders were tense when he spoke to T.J.

Mina didn't know it, but sometime during Brody and Savannah's discussion, she had left her seat to stand with her hands pressed against the window's glass, trying to reach through to be as close to Brody as possible. The pain of knowing love and losing it was almost too much for her to bear. She breathed his name under her breath and was startled when Brody looked across the courtyard right at her.

There was no way he could have heard her whisper his name, was there? Brody's frown turned farther down, and his brows furrowed in confusion. Mina froze and then realized how silly she must look half pushed against the glass, staring at him like some kind of lovesick puppy. She let out a squeak and dropped her hands to her sides.

Brody looked at Mina and then at the back of Savannah's retreating form, and shook his head. He turned, opened the door to the aquatics building, and stormed back inside. T.J. jumped in surprise at Brody's sudden change in mood and followed quickly behind.

Mina's cheeks burned with embarrassment, and she looked back at the door that Brody had just entered. He'd looked at her! He'd actually stopped and met her eyes. His reaction was not what she expected. A painful imaginary orb lodged in her throat, making it hard to swallow, and her heart broke a little more for her once-upon-a-time boyfriend.

It wasn't that long ago that she found out that her name was not Mina Grime but Mina Grimm, and she was descended from the Brothers Grimm. Her mother had changed their name and moved constantly, trying to hide from the Story. But it didn't matter; it had still found them. Mina was now tasked with completing hundreds of fairy tale quests in order to end a generational curse on her family.

Her first fairy tale quests had been the most challenging. She had imprisoned an ageless Fae named Claire, defeated a wolf pack, and saved her best friend's life. All while secretly dating the hottest and most popular guy in school. But their whole relationship, the whole experience was gone. Completely forgotten — this was a horrible side effect of her curse. Apparently, the Story, to protect itself and the Fae from humans, could erase memories and alter events. And it did, to Mina's horror, and she lost her boyfriend and the few blissful weeks they had been together.

Her mother, Sara, had tried to explain it to her. "Well, honey, it's similar to walking somewhere and being lost in thought, and all of a sudden you arrive at your destination with no recollection of the journey. Your mind fills in the blanks, and it will fill it in with what is the most plausible scenario."

"What does he think happened?" Mina asked in desperation.

"He thinks whatever the Story pushes him toward thinking. If he normally would have gone home after school each day, then that is what he did. Honey, at your age, hundreds of your days are so similar and repetitive that it is easy for the Story to make us believe we lived the same pattern over and over again."

Mina's lip quivered as she whispered, "It's not fair!"

Sara reached over to her daughter and pulled her into a hug. "There's no such thing as fair when it comes to the Fae and their tales."

"Will he ever remember, Mom? Will he ever remember the dance, the rides to school? Will he ever remember he kissed me?" It was becoming too much for her to fathom.

"Sweetie, the Fae are powerful, and so is the Story that drives all of the Grimms' futures. But let me tell you that nothing is more powerful than true love. And until you find out whether he is your true love or not, I can tell you from experience that those caught in the Story's web will have intense moments of déjà vu. So don't give up."

And that was exactly what Mina had been hoping for — a chance, a glimpse, something that would spur a moment of enlightenment — and then he would turn to her, take her in his arms, and say, "I remember!" But after a few days of awkward and confused glances, Mina began to think it wasn't going to happen.

"He must think I'm some sort of creeper," Mina mumbled under her breath.

"Um, yeah, he probably does," Nan answered.

Mina was startled by her friend's voice. She had become oblivious to Nan and hadn't noticed when she came and sat on the desk next to her to stare out the window at Brody.

Nan took a sucker out of her mouth and pointed the sticky ball at her friend. "You, dear Mina, need to get a life."

Mina's eyes crossed as she took in the wet, red, candy ball on a stick. "Where did you get that?"

Nan rolled her eyes and pulled three more out of her purse. "I'm trying to lay off the cupcakes. Too many dyes. So I switched vices. Want one?" She fanned the suckers and waved them enticingly in front of Mina.

"No, thanks."

"It wouldn't solve your problem anyway!" Nan spoke with the sucker still in her mouth.

"What problem?" Mina asked, slightly confused.

"The one where you're turning into a square." She held up her pointer fingers and thumbs to create a square and looked through it at Mina.

"Compared to what? Are you saying I wasn't one before?"

Nan turned her head to the side. "Well, you always were more of a triangle. But ever since the dance, you've been different." She pointed a thumb at the aquatics building. "Is it because of Brody that you're so broody? Ha! I made a joke…get it?"

Mina turned back toward her desk and put her books into her new backpack. She paused as she remembered a similar backpack with safety pins holding it together. Her mind was flooded with images of Brody falling, her reaching out and grabbing his backpack and saving his life, and all of the days after. The onslaught of memories made Mina frustrated, so she violently tossed the books into her bag.

She needed to quit living in the past and start worrying about her future. Who knew how long it would be before the Story gathered power and unleashed another fairy tale quest on her?

"Okay, I'm a square and I need a life. What do you, O Wise One, suggest?" Mina tried to smile and play along.

Nan pulled out her iPhone and started typing. "Next weekend the hottest band is playing, and I am determined to get tickets to the show."

Mina groaned aloud. "Don't tell me it's that band that sounds like screeching cats? What are they called? Um, Royal Flush, King's Council?"

Nan pouted. "They do not sound like screeching cats. And they're called the Dead Prince Society. I'll stand in line all night if I have to, but we are definitely going. And we definitely need to find you different clothes."

"What's wrong with my clothes?" Mina looked down at her vintage striped shirt and grimaced at the obvious paint stain from her earlier art project. What others called thrift store, Mina's mom called vintage. How could she have missed the stain? She furiously rubbed at the offending paint and it started to slowly chip off, but it was going to take a lot of chipping to get it all.

She'd thought she'd been doing better with her wardrobe. At least she no longer wore hoodie jackets, which had tended to be a bane to her on her last encounter with the Story, when it had tried to turn her into Red Riding Hood and made all of her clothes red. Still, it was tough to fit in and buy expensive clothes when her single mom, who cleaned houses for a living, supported her and her brother. So Mina chose to wear hand-me-down, garage-sale items and thrift-store finds, which weren't all bad.

"Forget it, Mina. The shirt is a lost cause. It's not worth salvaging." Nan grabbed her hand, pulled her out of the chair. Mina sighed, picked up her backpack, and followed her friend out into the hall of Kennedy High.

Most of the students had already left for the day, and only those who had detention or were involved in after-school clubs and sports were on campus. Mina never minded staying late after school. It meant she was able to see Brody and avoid running into despicable Jared.

Mina had once believed Jared was dead, and had felt responsible for his death. A Fae wolf had jumped from a moving van onto Jared's motorcycle while they were both speeding down a highway. Mina saw them crash, and she believed there was no way they could have survived that wreck. She had been devastated and spent days crying over him. Now, since he obviously wasn't dead, she wished he was. He was rude, obnoxious, and a complete jerk.

The day that Jared had appeared in the school lunchroom, miraculously alive, would be forever burned into her memory. For a moment, when he'd surprised her and looked at her with such heat-filled and intense eyes, one would have thought it was Mina who had almost died. She'd clutched the table for support and dug her nails into it so she wouldn't run to him crying and blubbering loudly. He'd seen her slight movement and given just the slightest head shake "no." He'd continued to stare right into her soul as he moved across the lunchroom to sit at a different table. Jared was rejecting her, to keep up with appearances of being a new student.

Mina's heart had thudded. She'd heard her blood rushing in her ears as she'd tried to make sense of the intense emotions that had overtaken her at the sight of Jared and his immediate response to her. Excitement, happiness, joy, confusion, hurt, betrayal, sadness — all of those emotions had flushed across her face in a blink of an eye, and she'd sat down hard on the chair. Nan had barely noticed as she had droned on and on about the new kid.

Mina hadn't been able to take the rejection from the one person who knew who she really was. And obviously Jared still remembered everything that had happened. Why? Why would he do this to her? She'd sat numbly across the room from

Jared, who knew her but pretended otherwise, and Brody, who didn't remember her and she wished had. The Fates were cruel. Why couldn't it have been the opposite? Why couldn't Brody have retained his memories and Jared have forgotten?

Mina had felt awful at her sudden change of thought and covered her face with her hands. It was too much, all too much for a sixteen-year-old to absorb. It wasn't until she'd heard Savannah White's laugh fill the lunchroom that Mina had officially lost it. She'd grabbed her tray and pushed it across the lunch table, then stood up loudly as her chair had flipped over, causing every head to turn her way expectantly. Every head except for Jared's.

Mina had been angry. Angrier than she'd felt in a while. As a result, she'd turned and pushed another chair out of the way. The chair had moved effortlessly, and magically it changed directions. It skidded into a poor passerby, Steven. He stumbled and dropped his lunch tray of food right into the lap of the one and only Savannah White. Savannah had screamed at Steven and his pile of spaghetti that spilled across her pristine cheerleader uniform. The lunchroom erupted into laughter.

Mina had stood and stared at the domino effect she had caused and couldn't believe her luck. She'd looked at the faces of the students. No one had even looked at her or noticed her actions. Savannah's angry tirade became louder and more hysterical. Mina had glanced one more time toward Jared, and he'd purposefully looked down at his tray with a smug grin across his face. His eyes almost couldn't contain the obvious mischief that lurked there.

That had explained it all. Mina wasn't sure how she'd known, but Jared was behind the mysteriously moving chair, and the Steven and Savannah spectacle. She'd wondered if it was some kind of peace offering for refusing to acknowledge her. Well, she hadn't taken it. Mina had turned and walked out the double doors of the lunchroom, leaving the monkey house it had become behind.

That had been over a month ago. Still Jared hadn't spoken to her. And Brody had just been giving her odd looks. Boy trouble, plus the intense pressure of always trying to be on her guard for the next quest, was taking a toll on her nerves. She could feel her younger self starting to slip away to be replaced by a forlorn, lovesick, paranoid loony. Mina felt like she was floating above herself and looking down, not actually participating in her life.

"WATCH OUT!" Nan screamed.

Mina felt a strong tug on her green corduroy jacket, and she was jerked back onto the curb and into the present. A red convertible carrying a bunch of screaming teenage girls whizzed by, almost running over her. She looked up in confusion at her surroundings. They were standing outside Kennedy High School next to the curb across from the parking lot. When had they walked outside? Was she really zoning out into her own thoughts so much that she was losing big chunks of time? She didn't even remember walking across the campus.

Nan released her death grip on Mina's jacket. "Mina, really. Please tell me what is wrong with you."

The adrenaline of almost getting hit by a car started to overtake her. If Nan hadn't been right next to her, she would've been toast. Burnt toast, crispy, not even worth salvaging, and where would that leave her family? It would've meant that Charlie, her silent younger brother, would be the next Grimm to face the Story.

She was not meant to go out like that, not by something as simple as walking into oncoming traffic. How in the world was she going to face another dangerous quest when she couldn't even keep herself safe? She began to feel dizzy, sick, and nauseous all at once. Her legs became Jell-O, and they buckled beneath her. She crumpled to the sidewalk, breathing heavily.

Nan screamed her name, and a buzzing noise filled Mina's ears. She could've sworn she heard Claire's evil laugh echoing around her and heard LoneTree snarling at her.

Another car pulled up next to them and a window rolled down. "What's going on? What happened?"

The strong voice broke through the echo of Claire's maniacal laugh in her head, but Mina still couldn't calm her breathing or her heart.

Nan answered, "She was almost hit by a car, and I think she's in shock."

"Don't move." A car door opened, footsteps came around, and another door opened. Mina was so dazed she let Nan usher her into the back seat of the car with little resistance.

The feel of cool leather seats brushed against Mina's face, and the smell was oddly familiar, though unrecognizable. Three car doors slammed and the engine roared to life.

"Where to?" the male driver asked.

Mina looked around the back seat of the car. A few textbooks and a black sports bag with the school's mascot and water polo silhouette in white were the only things littering the floor. She looked up into the rearview mirror, and concerned blue eyes met hers. She didn't need to see the driver's face to know that she was in the back seat of Brody Carmichael's car.

"972..." Nan rattled off.

"NO!" Mina yelled out a little too loudly. Nan was giving Brody her home address.

Nan's head whipped around from the front seat to stare at her wide-eyed. "So you don't want to go home? I thought you were having some kind of breakdown back there."

Mina bit her lip and looked down in embarrassment. "I'm okay now. The shock of almost being hit by the car stunned me for a bit. I'm fine…really," she added lamely.

Nan's eyebrow rose, firmly stating she didn't quite believe her. "Whatever." She opened the car door and stepped out onto the curb. "I guess we won't need a ride after all."

Brody answered, "It's fine. I can give you a lift anywhere you want to go." His wet hair had almost dried from the sun. Mina wanted to reach out and touch the semi-wet locks, but pulled back. She briefly wondered if he'd been as confused and conflicted as she was lately.

Mina pulled on the back door's handle, but it didn't budge; it was still locked. She couldn't believe it, child-proof locks.

Brody turned his head to stare at Mina, who was latched onto the door handle, waiting to leap out of the car as soon as he unlocked it. He didn't. He watched and waited for what seemed like an eternity before asking, "What are you doing this weekend?" Even though the question was obviously directed at Mina, it was Nan who answered from the sidewalk.

"We are going to see Dead Prince Society. I suppose you wouldn't know who they are, would you?"

Brody's eyes shifted toward Mina before answering. "Yeah, I know them. The lead singer is my cousin."

"WHAT! I can't believe it! Valdemar is your cousin. That is about the coolest thing ever. Can you get us autographs?" Nan was in rock heaven.

He looked toward Nan's dancing form as she jumped around, waving her hands in anticipation. Brody's mouth turned upward before he looked at Mina again in the back seat.

"I'll do you one better. Let me drive you there Saturday, and I'll get you backstage passes."

Even more screaming erupted from Nan, causing a nearby flock of birds to fly off. Mina covered her ears in surprise. Brody winced in pain.

"YES, yes, holy mackerel, yes." She began to sing out loud the chorus to their latest hit song, "Beauty's Dead." She quickly became oblivious to Mina's plight at being still locked in the car.

"What about you, Mina?" Brody asked, his voice growing softer.

Her fingers reluctantly let go of the door handle. She couldn't bring herself to look him in the eyes.

"All right," she whispered.

What was wrong with her? This was what she had been waiting for, a chance to reunite with Brody, to see if what they had was real, or if it was a product of the Story's manipulation. As much as she longed for Brody, there was the remote possibility that without the Story's interference, he might not feel the same way about her again. Was she ready to try again and risk losing him? YES!

Brody blinked in surprise. Apparently she had spoken aloud and with force.

"Okay, then, it's settled." He reached for the automatic lock and pushed the button, releasing Mina from the back seat.

Before she stepped out, she asked him, "Would you have unlocked the door if I had said no?"

"Possibly. We won't really know, now, will we? Since you didn't — say no, that is." His lips pressed together, and he smiled crookedly. He touched his forehead and squeezed his eyes. With a slight shake of his head, he started the car and waited as Mina exited the back seat. She could tell that he was struggling with something inside himself, some memories. It only made Mina's heart break for him a little bit more.

"Where should we meet you?" Nan smiled and leaned in the opened window.

Brody looked at Mina when he said, "How about I pick you up at — "

"Nan's condo!" Mina interrupted, knowing exactly what Brody was going to suggest. She learned her lesson the first time; she wanted to keep him far away from her mother. Mina didn't want any more arguments or "I told you so"s in case things didn't go her way again.

Brody frowned, but entered Nan's address in his phone anyway. "I'll pick you up at six."

The sound of a motorcycle revving made Mina's head snap up. The timing was inconceivable. Jared was once again on his black motorcycle across the street. He revved the engine again, intentionally drawing attention to himself. Mina glared at him, and he shook his head slowly, telling her no.

Her eyes widened in disbelief. There was no way he knew what she was thinking of doing? He couldn't have overheard their conversation about going to the concert. Or could he?

Angry and frustrated, she put on her most flirtatious smile, which probably looked awkward and pained. But Mina did her best to impersonate Savannah. "Oh, I can't wait. It will be so much fun." Mina smiled and stuck her chin up in the air, in a challenge to Jared, daring him to stop her.

To show his displeasure, he hit the gas and front brakes, causing a very long circular skid of rubber along the pavement as he did a one-eighty and tore off down the road.

Nan wrinkled her nose at the smell of burning rubber. Brody waved before driving away.

"What was that?" Nan asked accusingly.

"What was what?" Mina said in her most innocent voice.

"Oh, you can't fool me." Nan switched to a high-pitched voice. "Oh, golly gee whiz, Brody. It will be so much fun. Can't wait." Nan wiggled her head back and forth, making her blonde hair swish in an exact parody of Savannah. Mina was momentarily stunned by how close the similarity was.

"Gosh, Mina," Nan huffed out. "Want to make him run the other way fast? Just start talking like his ex-girlfriend."

"I wasn't purposefully trying to." Mina's shoulders dropped in discouragement. "I was trying to channel someone fun and flirty, and she was the first person to pop into my head."

"What! I wasn't the first one you thought of? I'm offended. I'm way more fun and flirty than Savannah."

She had a point. Nan was one of the prettiest girls in the school and had a fun, flirty attitude. Everyone knew who Nan Taylor was; her divorced parents were lawyers and wealthy to boot.

And if they didn't personally know her, they probably followed her on Twitter, or whatever the latest social media craze was. She could quite possibly be the most popular girl in school, if she ever tried. But Nan didn't try; she didn't try to fit in or be anything other than who she was, and for that Mina was grateful.

A familiar tingling sensation began crawling up Mina's spine, a warning that something Fae or magical was near. She turned around and looked for the source of her discomfort.

Nan was still talking as Mina bit her lip in worry. She scanned the students hanging around. There were a few underclassmen doing tricks on skateboards and Principal Hame was sauntering over to begin yelling at them; Savannah and Pri were showing off a new cheer to a group of girls. Everything looked ordinary, even down to the small-boned, pale-skinned girl listening to her iPod near the fence. She was new, or at least Mina had never seen her before. She was beautiful in an intense sort of way. Her hair was short and fashionably unruly. Her pleated skirt and vest resembled a private school uniform, except for the very loud shoes. A deliberate style choice, no doubt.

Mina was about to ignore the feeling of power and trepidation when the girl looked up from her iPod and made eye contact with her. Barely contained loathing flickered across the girl's face. Mina called Nan's name and turned to ask her about the new student. But when they both looked back, the girl was gone.

CHAPTER 3

It was five o'clock, and Mina still hadn't found anything out of Nan's closet to wear. Mainly because Nan was trying to dress Mina up like a doll. The other reason was that Nan's room was more of a disaster zone than Mina's. Mina's room looked messy. Nan's looked like a bomb went off in it.

"Ooh, this one's nice." Nan pulled out a blue and white long shirt and held it up for her best friend's inspection. "Paired with a gold belt and my brown boots, it would be to die for."

Mina nodded. "And with those jeans," she said.

Nan stared at Mina in disbelief. "You can't wear pants with this! It's a dress." She pulled the dress shirt up to her own body and modeled it. "See, a dress."

Mina made a face. "No, that is half a dress!"

Nan flounced around the room and pulled out three more dress shirts in similar fashion. "See, they are a shirt and a dress. It's the latest fashion." She pouted at Mina, and held them out for her to pick one.

"Fashion for a Barbie, maybe? I couldn't possibly wear it."

"You never know until you try." Nan rolled her eyes.

"No, I know I will never try it on." Mina chuckled good-naturedly.

"Wilhelmina Grime, you go in there and try this on…NOW!" Nan tossed the dress at Mina and physically pushed her into her own en suite bathroom.

"No, ack! No…stop!" Mina screamed and tried to argue, but couldn't as Nan began to assault her with accessories and the other shirt dresses. Giving in, Mina took the clothes and retreated to the bathroom. Nan's bathroom was larger than Mina's small bedroom, with a garden-soaking tub, dual sinks, and a shower that had a waterfall feature.

Mina sighed and laid the dresses across the cluttered counter, on an area that had less mess. Stripping down, she tried a long emerald green shirt and was impressed. It fell slightly above her knees, shorter than anything she owned. But it didn't look inappropriate. She knew if she were any taller, it would show way too much leg. She added a gold belt, bangles, and a necklace, and slipped on a pair of Steve Madden boots.

Nan peeked her head in the bathroom. "Wow! You are definitely wearing that one." She picked up a brush and began to braid Mina's hair into a loose fishtail over one shoulder. Slightly pulling Mina's hair away from her face transformed her into a much older-looking girl. A quick dab of blush, lip gloss, and eye liner turned her into a young woman.

Mina looked at herself in the mirror and couldn't help but notice the beautiful girl staring back at her. She looked older, rich, and confident. But it was only because of Nan's clothes, Nan's makeup, and Nan's jewelry. For once, Mina was a little jealous of Nan. Yes, Mina had always been in awe of Nan, but she was so approachable, humble, and giving that there was never any room for jealousy.

But there was something more to it than money, Mina realized. She was jealous of Nan's ignorance. She didn't have a family curse hanging over her head threatening to take away her life. She reached over and turned the gold-plated faucet on, letting cold water run over her shaking hands. She got a drink and then splashed some on her face.

"Come on, Mina, snap out of it," she told herself over and over. Maybe it was just nerves about tonight's concert and that Brody Carmichael was going to be there any minute.

Nan wore a pair of black skinny jeans, layered lace tank tops, and what couldn't be less than ten bracelets on one arm. She took less time with her own hair and makeup. When they stood in front of the mirror, Mina was the obvious beauty who stood out and shone like a star. It wasn't until later that night that she realized her best friend had purposely dressed down.

They walked into the open concept kitchen and raided the stainless-steel fridge, looking for snacks to pass the time. The fridge was practically empty. A few bottles of water, ketchup, Greek yogurt, and oranges looked lonely on the glass shelves. Normally, something like this would worry Mina. But she knew the Taylors hardly ever ate at home, and usually ordered in all of their food.

Nan handed Mina a yogurt and bottled water as the elevator dinged and two people stepped out into the living room. A high ringing laugh echoed around the condo as Mrs. Taylor sauntered into the room. Her hair was bleached an unnatural shade of white blonde. Her expensive suit jacket was thrown over her purse, and her usual silk blouse was replaced by a lacy shirt obviously out of her daughter's closet. All signs that pointed to a woman trying to act younger than she was. The reason was the tall, dark, and handsome man beside her who was adoringly hanging on every word she spoke. They embraced and kissed.

Gagging sounds came from Nan's direction, and Mina turned to find her friend making grotesque faces at her mother and the good-looking man, Robert Martin, who was to be her future stepfather. Mina had heard all of the stories.

Apparently Nan's mom, Veronica, had met him when they both accidentally jumped into the same cab. He was going to get out and let her have the cab, but then he offered to pay for both of their fares, if he were allowed to ride with her and enjoy her company. Of course, any single, hardworking woman, who had been without a beau for a long time, couldn't refuse the offer. The rest was history. Two weeks later they were officially dating; two months later, engaged.

Now they were planning a wedding so big it was going to blow Veronica's first wedding to Nan's father out of the water.

Mina decided to ask Nan what she thought of her new future stepdad.

She shrugged, "He's fine, I guess. That is if you like them tall, dark, and *boring*," Nan muttered

"What does he do again?" Mina asked, taking a drink of her bottled water while eyeing the love-struck adults whispering to each other in the next room.

"He's a doctor for the new hospital. You know, the one that is completely made of glass."

Mina did know which hospital Nan was referring to. It was just finished a few months ago and was state of the art in design and facilities.

"That's cool," Mina countered, feeling somewhat at a loss. She wasn't sure how to console her friend. Nan's only complaint about her mom's new boyfriend was usually stuff like "he is boring" and "too perfect" and obviously "not her dad."

Robert Martin gave Veronica a quick kiss on her cheek as she went down the hall, and he headed toward the kitchen.

"What's up, Nan?" Robert asked.

"The ceiling!" Nan retorted. Mina started laughing.

Robert completely ignored Nan's snide comment. "So have you considered what your mom said about Harvard?"

Nan dug her spoon into her yogurt forcefully, stirring it with a vengeance. "Did she consider what I said about Julliard?"

"Don't worry about the argument with your mom the other night. We have some time. If that is where you would like to go after high school, I'll make it happen." He opened a cupboard and found some trail mix. He began popping the peanuts into his mouth, crunching them loudly.

Nan became a little sullen. "Yeah, okay." She didn't look up at Robert when he offered her some trail mix. Undeterred, he swung the open bag toward Mina, who took a handful.

"So, I was thinking. I have a cabin up on Imperial Lake. Your mom and I can take my new boat up there, and you can invite some of your friends for a lake party. How's that sound?

Nan's mood immediately brightened. "I can invite whoever I want?"

Robert shrugged. "Sure, why not?'

Nan tried but couldn't hide the enthusiasm on her face. "That sounds awesome! When?"

"How about in two weeks?" Robert chuckled, raising his hands in surrender. He looked pleased with the sudden turnaround in Nan's disposition.

She jumped off the stool she had been perched on, tossed her empty yogurt cup in the garbage, gave a little twirl, and pointed her little finger at Robert. "Pinky swear."

The tall dark-haired doctor gave in to Nan's exuberance. He held out his pinky and they shook.

"It's a date, for me and my friends. No take-backs." She scrunched up her face and challenged him to say otherwise.

"No take-backs. I promise." He smiled.

The elevator dinged again, and everyone's head turned toward the doors expectantly. When they opened, Brody stepped out. Mina felt all of the oxygen get sucked from the room. Or that's what it felt like, since she'd forgotten to breathe. He wore simple jeans and a button-down white shirt, but the way he wore them made them seem extremely stylish. He looked around the expansive living room and took in all of the inhabitants in one quick motion. His face lit up when he saw them in the kitchen.

"You ready?" Brody sauntered over to them with his hands in his jean pockets.

Robert scowled at Brody. "Ready for what?"

Brody looked somewhat taken aback by the attack, but he countered easily with a knock 'em dead grin.

"For the concert tonight. I've got backstage passes." He held out his hand toward Robert and introduced himself.

Robert stared at Brody before finally giving in and shaking his hand. He turned toward Nan, and he began to lose his casual demeanor.

"Concert. You didn't mention anything about a concert tonight. Or that you would be going with boys." He tried to sound neutral, but it came off as being overprotective.

"Lay off, Robert," Nan shot out. "I already cleared it with my *MOM*." Her tone left no room for argument; it purposely reminded him that he wasn't her father, at least not yet. Robert's mouth opened and closed like a fish. Nan didn't give anyone time to respond before she grabbed her purse and headed toward the elevator. Mina quickly followed, and Brody tipped his head in farewell before trailing after them.

When the elevator closed and they began the twenty-three-floor descent, Mina couldn't help but feel claustrophobic being so close to Brody. Nan tapped her foot to the music of Seven String Quartet coming over the elevator speakers while pulling out her phone to text someone. Brody leaned against the wall, looking them over.

"You both look nice," he said quietly. He looked at Nan and then Mina.

Mina's eyes lifted for a moment and caught his. Her cheeks burned, and she could only whisper the word, "Thanks."

Where was her resolve to be charming and confident? It had disappeared the moment he walked into the room. She could smell his cologne, and she had to concentrate just to breathe.

Nan turned around, raised her eyebrows toward Brody, and gave Mina a knowing smile when he wasn't looking. They left the lobby and walked out to Brody's SUV. Nan immediately slid into the back seat, forcing Mina to take the front. The twenty-minute drive to the concert was filled with Nan's constant chatter about Dead Prince Society. How many tours they went on a year, which song was her favorite. Brody jumped in with all sorts of little-known facts.

Nan gushed about how cute Valdemar was, while leaning between the seats to put their CD into Brody's stereo. They started to sing out the words to the song "Beauty's Dead," and when their voices blended perfectly, they laughed at each other and Nan hit his shoulder.

Feeling somewhat pressured and left out, Mina blurted out the only thing she could think of. "Did you know that Valdemar isn't his real name?"

Brody laughed out loud, "Yeah, I called him Peter growing up."

"Oh, right, I forgot, cousins and all." Mina wanted to crawl into the cracks of the leather seat and disappear. Thankfully, Nan stepped in again and pulled the attention away from Mina.

"Thank goodness! I don't think Peter is a good name for the lead singer. Valdemar sounds much more mysterious."

Mina hung back and let Nan and Brody banter back and forth the rest of the car ride, which thankfully, was almost over. They were able to find a parking spot within a few blocks' walk of the venue. Brody walked up to the will call booth and gave his name.

An overly plump man in a black tank top with a dragon tattoo on his arm made a quick call on his phone. He nodded and handed them three vinyl tags on lanyards. "Don't lose these and don't sell 'em," he grumbled.

Brody handed out the backstage passes. Nan could barely contain her excitement as the man got off his worn stool in the small booth and led them to a metal side door. He knocked, and what looked like a bodyguard opened the door. The bodyguard and ticket attendant spoke in low tones before motioning them forward.

Not really knowing what to expect, Mina stuck to Nan's side like glue. They walked down a back hallway and were directed toward an elevator. After taking the elevator up, they walked out into a large open room filled with couches, food, makeup artists, photographers, and fans.

"Where are we?" Mina asked in hushed tones.

"The green room," Nan said in awe.

Mina looked at the floor and walls. "But it's not green."

Nan's neck snapped back and forth like a metronome as she took in the surroundings. "It's just called that. It's the hangout room for special guests and the rock stars before and after they perform. I can't believe it." She squeezed Mina's hand in excitement and pointed when she caught sight of one of the band members.

Naga was Japanese and wore head-to-toe black leather with matching boots. He even had a spiked mohawk tipped with white. He was clearly upset about something and was visibly arguing with his hairstylist. Mina could only guess that it had something to do with the very skunk-like turn his hair was taking.

Brody was talking to a young man with white-blond hair pulled into a ponytail who was the epitome of a punked-out version of Lord of the Rings' Legolas. Nan whispered Constantine's name in awe to Mina. "After Valdemar, he is the second hottest Prince in the band. You do remember what I told you, right? That each of them chose their stage name after an actual dead prince?"

The third band member was the largest and sat stuffing his face from the vast array of sandwiches, snacks, and fruit on a table. It was interesting that all the healthy food sat untouched while the floor was littered with bags of opened candy. Mina wished she had spent more time learning the names of the band members, or at least their stage names. For some reason she kept thinking his name was Magpie — no, Martin—ah, wait…Magnus. Too nervous to stare at the fiercely intimidating guy for any length of time, she kept glancing to the others in the room, trying to guess who the other member was.

"Oh, I can't believe this is happening! No one on earth is going to believe this. Here, take my phone. Get a picture of me next to Valdemar," Nan hissed.

A solemn young man with golden hair down to his chin, wearing skintight jeans and a black vest, sat on a red vinyl couch, re-stringing his guitar. He appeared to be trying to ignore an over-exuberant female fan with bright pink hair.

"Which one is that again?" Mina asked, already forgetting the names Nan had pointed out earlier.

Nan tossed her the phone and went over to delicately sit on the edge of the red vinyl couch, feet away from the Dead Prince Society's lead singer. Nan nervously pasted a smile on her face and posed.

Unsure of what to do, it took Mina a few moments to figure out what Nan wanted. She got the phone to the right screen, but she couldn't get Nan and the rocker in the same shot. Mina motioned with her hands for Nan to scoot closer.

Nan's confidence faltered. Her smile slipped a little as she carefully slid inches closer to the rocker. It wasn't close enough. Mina mouthed the word "closer," and Nan scooted even closer to Valdemar, who seemed oblivious to Nan's inching. The girl with the bubblegum pink hair started to shoot them both nasty glances, but they ignored her.

Just when Nan had inched as close as she dared, Valdemar reached his arm out and quickly pulled her into his lap. She screeched in surprise, but was quieted as Valdemar's hands reached around her possessively, then was even more surprised when he leaned in and kissed her.

Mina snapped the picture.

CHAPTER 4

Nan was too stunned to fight or pull away from the kiss, and she let Valdemar continue. The girl with the pink hair looked furious and screamed something incoherent at the kissing couple. When she didn't get the immediate reaction she desired, she stormed out of the room, knocking over chairs and lamps in the process. When the exit door slammed with finality, Valdemar gently pulled away from the kiss. He looked momentarily surprised by his own reaction to the intensity of the shared kiss. It took him a minute to recover before he slid Nan onto the cushion next to him, closer than what was necessary.

"Sorry about that. I was at my wit's end trying to make her go away. Thank you for playing along." He glanced at the door and smirked, and turned back to Nan. "It worked at least." His eyes still held a hint of desire, and he swallowed nervously.

Nan perched awkwardly on the cushion next to him, her hand gently brushing her lips where they were seconds ago pressed to his. Her cheeks turned bright red, and she looked like she was at a loss for words. Hastily she jumped up from the couch, knocking her knee into the coffee table, trying to run away.

Valdemar's hand shot out and caught Nan's wrist. "Ah, I'm sorry. Please don't run away, I'd like..." He never got to finish his sentence, as a short fiery red-haired woman in a business suit entered the room and started ushering people out for the concert, which should have started five minutes ago.

The room became a mass of hurriedly fleeing flashes and last-minute fixes by the hair and makeup crew. Mina watched as Valdemar tried to speak to Nan again but was pulled away out the door to the stage. She was sure she saw him motion for Nan to stay there.

When Nan's blonde head swung forcefully back and forth in denial, his face dropped. But Mina could have been mistaken in what she saw, because Valdemar immediately plastered a smile on his face and headed toward stage. They followed. Three of the band members headed underneath the stage. It was dark, but they had enough light to see a lift and hydraulics. Valdemar split off and headed toward another contraption and a crowd of techs.

From her spot in the wings Mina had a phenomenal view of the stage and the packed house. Suddenly, the whole arena went dark. Smoke billowed out from fog machines hidden along the platform, and a low rumbling of music began. Somewhere, an organ began a somber melody, something that would be played at a funeral. Eerie sound effects and footsteps echoed off the walls, and only those backstage could hear the hydraulics kick in when the lift began to rise to the stage.

The hair on the back of Mina's neck stood up in anticipation when the stage props and band slowly rose into view. The band's stage was decorated like a dark and twisted throne room; a large golden mirror hung on the back wall. High in the middle of the stage sat a black throne made from a dark and twisted tree. Upon the throne sat a guitar painted in the deepest blood red color. Three of the band members were onstage playing the intro to their most popular song, "Beauty's Dead." Naga on the guitar, Magnus on drums, Constantine on bass, but Valdemar was missing.

Mina's head craned to look around the stage, her fear overtaking her as the dreaded feeling of magic began to tingle down her hands. A sign that the Story was interested in what was currently going on, and might even find a way to interfere.

Unexpectedly, the music stopped, and Nan screamed in delight and pointed toward the large golden mirror, which was filling with fog. The sound of a lone guitar picked up where the haunting melody had ended, and the fog began to clear from the mirror. Valdemar was inside the giant looking glass playing a gold guitar.

The crowd chanted as Valdemar ceased his playing and used his very expensive guitar to smash through the glass. Mina stepped away from the stage subconsciously as Valdemar stepped through the mirror. Their movements were eerily similar but polar opposite. The closer he moved to the stage, the farther Mina moved into the background and away from Brody and Nan.

She could feel it. Deep in her soul, lingering in her bones, she could feel the Story's power hovering. It was only a matter of time before it started, twisting and using what she had just seen, heard, and done into a quest. Her mouth went dry, and she started to shake with fear.

Valdemar raised his hands high into the air, and the audience and Nan jumped up and down in excitement. He strode over to the black throne and picked up the blood-red guitar and continued with the rest of their music set.

Why couldn't she have paid more attention? There were signs, obvious ones now that she thought about it. The name of the band, for one, and their hit song was a fairy tale ballad; even the group's stage names were all things that would attract the Story into using them. Throw in the fact that Mina, a Grimm, had walked through the doors and into a giant trap. Her mind began to spin with all of the possible scenarios and outcomes, and nothing looked good. If she didn't want to get her friends involved with the Story, then she had to get her friends out of the concert. NOW.

The song came to a crescendo. The band quit playing, and everyone sang the chorus a capella. Everyone except Mina. Brody had a grin on his face and seemed to be enjoying the music as well. He turned to look at her, gave her crooked smile, then turned back to watch his cousin sing. The smoke and vertigo lights lit up the stage and spilled over into the darkness where they stood, giving them the appearance of being in a dream.

She moved toward Nan but was jettisoned to the side when a group of stagehands rushed in, rolling out carts with large pyrotechnics displays. Mina moved back and bumped into another person, and became pinned between the rolling carts. The stagehands were moving fast, and Mina had no choice but to move with them or get run over. Fumbling to keep up and stay out of the way, Mina and the carts ended up down in the galley below the stage. They began to strap the contraptions onto the lift, and she could barely make out a large glass case off to the side.

She walked toward it and could see that it was easily six feet tall, but it was on its side and she didn't recognize what it was.

"What's that for?" she asked nervously.

One of the stagehands looked at her but went on with his work. He must not have heard her speak over the loud music. She decided to repeat herself loudly.

"What is that?" She waved and pointed toward the glass again.

This time he stopped briefly enough to answer her. "It's the glass coffin. We use it for the finale."

Mina turned in horror to look at the glass coffin that in fairy tales housed the body of a dead princess, the most famous one being Snow White. She took a deep breath and leaned closer. She could see her reflection staring back at her. Her own skin was pale with fear, her dark eyes wide with worry, and her lips looked red because she was biting them. She looked beautiful — that is, until she realized that her overlaid reflection gave the illusion that Mina was inside the glass coffin.

"NO!" she screamed, and jumped away from the cursed coffin. No one even heard her over the Dead Prince Society playing onstage.

Anger and fear filled her as the tingling sensation began to turn into waves. She could feel the power rolling off her, around her, into her.

"NO, I refuse! I refuse to play a part in this. Do you hear me, cursed Story? You don't own me. You don't get to choose what happens. It's not fair!" The music began to beat loudly in time with the waves of power and Mina grimaced in pain, clutching her ears.

She had to leave and leave now, with or without Nan and Brody. She rushed upstairs, ignoring the confused looks of the stagehands. She found Brody and Nan where she had left them.

"Nan, look, we need to go!" She tried to grab Nan, but her best friend violently pulled away from her.

"What do you mean, we have to go?" she asked in disbelief. "Didn't you see Valdemar? He wants me to stay here. There is going to be an after party. Brody, tell her!" Nan looked visibly upset at the prospect of leaving.

Brody looked back and forth between them, unsure of what to say. "Are you feeling all right? It's okay if we stay. My cousin cleared it. Nan's right — there is always a really cool after party. It's better than waiting in the green room."

Mina's lip was hurting from gnawing at it in panic. "No, I'm sorry. I just need...we just have to go."

"No, Mina, I'm not going. For the love of chocolate, I have been waiting all my life for this moment. He kissed me, Mina! He kissed me."

"You heard him. He said so himself. He did it to make the girl with the pink hair leave." Mina's voice filled with desperation.

"I don't care if it was because he was trying to make someone else jealous. I don't even care if it was a cruel and unusual jest on his part. I'm not walking away from that without pursuing it further. What if it wasn't a fluke? What if he actually kind of likes me? You want me to leave a very cool concert right now and go with you home because...."

"Because something bad is going to happen if we stay," Mina whispered. She peeked over her shoulder at Brody, who looked out of place, stuck between two girls fighting.

Nan's eyes widened.

Maybe, Mina thought, *maybe she will believe me.*

"How do you know?" Nan accused her angrily. "How can you possibly know?"

"I just do," Mina grumbled back.

"Well, that's not good enough." Nan stood there, silently challenging her. "Give me one good reason. Any *good* reason at all. Heck, it could be an even okay reason as long as you give me a real reason. Why?"

Mina could see the fight coming, and she was incapable of stopping it. She had never ever fought with her best friend, but then, they'd never ever had serious boyfriends until lately. It was then that Mina remembered that the kiss from Valdemar had been Nan's first kiss. Her boy-crazy, flirty, quirky friend had never been kissed. She knew Nan was waiting for the right one. And here she had found him, and Mina was trying to drag her away from him. Heat burned angrily in Nan's cheeks as Mina shook her head without giving her an answer.

Nan looked devastated. Her eyes began to water, and she looked like she was in pain. "That's fine, Mina. YOU can leave, but I'm staying for the after party."

"But I…" Mina's words and shoulders dropped dejectedly. She looked at Brody, embarrassed that he had witnessed their argument. She wasn't sure what he would do. Would he leave and come with her, or stay with Nan at the concert?

He looked deeply into Mina's eyes, and she felt her breath catch at the emotion she saw there. Surely he would come with her. He had to believe her. Maybe. Brody looked like he was about to say something when Nan interrupted him.

"Are you going to drag Brody out of the concert, too? Come on, Mina! It's his cousin, and they're on tour. How selfish are you going to be?"

Mina's resolve crumbled. She dropped her head toward the ground, hiding her shame and embarrassment. Nan's words had a biting truth to them. It was truth that she didn't want to hear acknowledged, but her friend was right. It would be rude to drag Brody out of here. Who was she? She was a nobody. She had no claim on Brody, no reason to make him come with her.

"I'm sure I can catch a bus or something. It's early enough." She turned to walk away from Nan. Her eyes burned with unshed tears, tears created by the pain they were causing each other.

She had originally told Nan about the curse on her family and all of the quests she had to complete. Her best friend had believed her. This time around Mina decided to not share it with Nan, in hopes that Nan wouldn't be caught up in Mina's personal mess. The loss of her best friend was devastating, the loss of trust even more so. She had only made it a few steps when Brody grabbed her by her elbow.

"Wait one minute. Okay?" He ran back to Nan, who stood with her back to them. Her posture was stiff, and he leaned in to whisper something to her. Nan's shoulders dropped and shook a bit, as if she was crying. A few seconds later, she stood up straight and regained her composure.

Brody ran over to Mina and followed her down the side stage stairs. They passed the glass coffin, and Mina felt a chill overtake her body just from looking at it. They had to go a few more corridors down, where the music wasn't so loud, before they were able to speak. When they were finally able to be heard over the music, Mina didn't have anything she wanted to say. Two turns later, she realized she was completely lost.

Brody chuckled, put his hand on the small of her back, and directed her down a different hallway. Her skin felt like it was on fire where he touched her back. It was warm and comforting as he led her toward the exit. When he opened up a side door to the parking lot, the cool breeze blew over her skin, and she shivered.

Stopping, Brody took off his jacket and put it around Mina's shoulders. Shocked and totally thrilled, Mina snuggled into the jacket and slyly inhaled the familiar scent of his cologne. Boy, did she have it bad for him. He opened the car door and let her slide inside. It was one of Brody's best attributes, his ability to always be the perfect gentleman.

It was still daylight out, and the sound of the concert could still be heard from inside the car. Brody fidgeted uncomfortably when he got in the car, delaying putting the key in the ignition.

"I'm sorry," he intoned sadly.

"For what?" Mina sniffled, trying to keep back the tears. "You didn't cause us to fight. What happened in there had nothing to do with you."

He reached for her hand and gently rubbed his thumb over the back of her fingers. "I'm sorry that you are hurting. It's because of me that you're even here in the first place. I offered to get those passes so I could get to know you. There's something about you that feels so comforting and familiar, and I'm not sure why." He pulled back abruptly from Mina and put both hands on the steering wheel as if he couldn't trust himself not to touch her.

Mina was elated at Brody's words, and she felt his absence as soon as he withdrew. How was he supposed to know that his body remembered touching her hand in this exact same manner, remembered kissing her, even if his mind couldn't?

Frustrated, she bit her lip again to keep herself from spilling forth secrets that she had promised to keep to herself forever. She had pledged not to involve those she loved anymore. They sat in awkward silence for moments more before he finally started the car and drove out of the parking lot.

"I'm sorry, too. Nan was right — it was unfair of me to go off like that. You don't have to drive me home. You should stay and enjoy the concert." Mina felt like the biggest, most selfish jerk in the world.

"Don't worry about it. I agreed to drive you both here, and I'll see that you get home safely." Brody turned to her, and his eyes softened. "Besides, I never liked their music anyway."

"Liar." She laughed out loud. "I saw you singing just as loudly as Nan. You like them."

"Okay, you caught me," he agreed. He gave her another glance out of the corner of his eye. "But I don't think I will miss much. I would rather be here."

Mina felt her knees go weak and her heart start to flutter wildly in her chest. What should she do? How should she respond? What should she say? She could feel the tension building up in the silence until she finally spat out the word, "Thanks." She immediately wanted to bash her head into the dashboard. Stupid, stupid, stupid. She was so stupid.

Even though her response was a complete junior higher's response, Brody still laughed. "You're welcome." He reached for the CD player and pushed "play" on the car stereo. The song picked up where they had left off, belting out the chorus to "Beauty's Dead." The song instantly reminded her of Nan, alone backstage at the concert.

She sighed. "I feel bad that we're abandoning Nan with no way to get home."

"We're not." Brody turned to look at Mina, a hint of redness on his cheeks. "I didn't feel comfortable leaving her there, either. Even though he's my cousin, Peter and his friends are not the most responsible. They tend to be a bit reckless. After I drop you off, I'm going to go back to the concert."

There was an ever-so-gentle flicker of disappointment. "Oh, I see," Mina lied. A sour taste crept into her mouth. She didn't see how Nan was willing to wait until after the concert to see the boy she liked. But at the same time, she was going to keep Mina from spending time with Brody.

She felt the stab of jealousy and could almost see it rear its ugly head in the tone of her own voice. "That is nice of you," she bit out.

Whatever beautiful moment they had shared moments ago was ruined by her own jealousy as she imagined the rest of the night playing out in fast forward: Brody, Nan, and all the band members would be laughing, eating bags of Skittles, and singing karaoke together. What? Where did that come from?

She tried to calm her nerves and remember where they were going. She was so distraught over the images her own mind had created that she didn't even care when she gave directions to her own house.

Brody was really quiet the rest of the drive, as if he could sense Mina's inner turmoil and dialogue. He cleared his throat gently when he pulled up in front of the Wongs' restaurant.

"You live in a Chinese restaurant?" Brody asked, unaware that he had already asked this question weeks ago and that he already subconsciously knew the answer.

An intense moment of déjà vu overcame Mina, and she turned to look at Brody and spoke slowly, watching his face closely for any hint of recognition. "Not in — above it." All of her waiting was for naught. He didn't react differently.

"Cool." He ran his hand through his hair and turned to look at her. "I'm sorry this night didn't turn out the way I had hoped."

Mina stepped out of the car. "No, it didn't," she mumbled back, feeling defeated until she remembered something. "Um, Nan's party at Imperial Lake next weekend. Are you going?" Her knees locked up, and she would have slapped herself in the forehead for how dorky she must have sounded if only he hadn't been standing next to her.

Brody pondered a minute as if checking an imaginary calendar in his head before answering with a grin, "Yeah, I got the invite, I wouldn't miss it."

Awkwardly, she waved goodbye, unsure of what else to do at this current stage of their non-existent dating status. She knew she was farther along in the relationship in her mind than he was. But it made her forget her spat with her best friend and even her current situation. Mina was floating on a cloud of hope.

Mrs. Wong was sweeping the front sidewalk to the restaurant. She waved enthusiastically at Mina as she went up the steps to the Grimes' apartment. It was obvious from Mrs. Wong's gestures that she wanted to speak to Mina and hear all of the juicy details involving the very attractive boy dropping her off. For some odd reason, she was obsessed with Mina's life and with giving her dating advice, even so far as to once suggest that Mina should kiss Brody. Thank goodness she had probably forgotten that embarrassing conversation had ever happened.

For once Mina was actually beginning to understand the reasoning behind the Story's resetting her life and the events occurring prior to the completion of a quest. In short, it did give her a second chance at first impressions. What high school student wouldn't want a chance to redo her first kiss, first dance, and biggest mistake?

She really hated what the Story had done and had become really depressed over losing her boyfriend. But at the same time, she was now free again to try to rekindle the flame without all of the previous awkwardness. The only thing to do now was to make absolutely sure that none of her friends, schoolmates, or boys she liked in the future ever became a part of the curse surrounding her, so she must make sure they never found out about it.

That was it; she would do everything she could to make sure they never had anything to do with the Story or her family's quests. If they weren't pulled into it, then their memories wouldn't be erased and their lives wouldn't be reset. It seemed simple enough.

Smiling, Mina managed the last few steps to the landing and inserted the key in the lock. She opened her door and stepped into her home. It wasn't much: a tiny retro kitchen with a '60s dinette set for four and appliances that had seen better days. A small sofa and wooden rocker filled up their very small living room along with an old TV, which was rarely used. Their apartment only had one bathroom, but luckily it did have three bedrooms, which was rare for their units. Well, Charlie's room wasn't legally a room, because he didn't have a closet and it looked as if it had originally been a part of Mina's room at one time. The previous tenants, or the Wongs at some point, must have built a wall between the two rooms to make a storage room or office. Either way, it had a window and gave the Grimes each enough privacy.

On the living room rug, Charlie was playing cards, what looked like a loose version of solitaire, but Mina could tell right away he was cheating. For one reason, she could see five aces and six queens, so there were obviously multiple decks in play, and he kept shuffling cards from the back to the front.

Mina chuckled, and Charlie looked up and made a loving brotherly face at her, which meant he scrunched up his nose and stuck out his tongue. Mina crossed her eyes and mimicked the tongue gesture. Charlie's face lit up in joyful glee at his sister's retaliation. Sara was making popcorn in the microwave and looked like she was getting ready to settle down with a good book. Mina said hi, snagged a handful of popcorn out of her mother's bowl, and retreated to her room with a quick comment about studying.

Once her door was closed, she grabbed a light jacket, purposely ignoring the various hoodies hanging in her closet. She clutched a small brown paper bag that she'd left on her desk, threw open her window, and stepped out onto the fire escape. The building was old and still had a rarely used fire escape, which led to Mina's rooftop retreat.

It was every teenager's dream to have a retreat of her own. It wasn't grand, but it was solely Mina's. The few lawn chairs that she had dragged up to the roof were mismatched and slightly broken dumpster finds, but she thought they were perfect. She had also decorated the roof with various fake plants, Christmas lights, outdoor party lights, and a lone pink flamingo. Faint music from the Italian restaurant down the road song drifted to her haven, and the mixed smells of Chinese and Italian food always created the oddest aroma of home.

She pulled out the crumpled paper bag and removed her latest curbside find, a medium-size garden gnome with blue pants and a red pointy hat. She wasn't sure what possessed her to save this somewhat chipped piece of clay, but it looked lonely. To be honest, she kind of felt sorry for the statue.

Twisting a stray lock of hair around her finger, she scanned the various ledges and shelves she had stacked with knickknacks and plants. She decided to place the gnome next to one of the few living plants on the roof, a rose bush. Placing him in his new home, Mina stood back and picked up a stick and pretended to knight the little fellow over both shoulders.

"I dub thee Sir Nomer," she said in a kingly tone of voice, her heart soaring.

"Well, that's a stupid name if I ever heard one myself, and I'm pretty sure I've heard lots of stupid names."

Mina froze at the male voice that seemed to come out of the air, and she stared at the garden gnome in disbelief. "Did you just say something?" she whispered to the gnome.

"Don't tell me you think the gnome can talk? Well, yes, some gnomes do talk. But most are surly and wouldn't really speak to you in the first place anyway, but certainly not cheap store-bought ones." The male voice spoke again and sounded closer. It only took Mina a second now to recognize the teasing tone of Jared's voice, and she stiffened in irritation.

"I happen to think that Nomer is a great name," Mina huffed out without looking at him.

"Obviously, it's for stupid dolls," Jared answered.

Mina turned around to confront Jared, but he wasn't standing behind her. Looking up, she frowned disapprovingly. "You should get down from there before you hurt yourself."

He was sitting on a brick outbuilding above her, wearing jeans and a green T-shirt. His dark hair ruffled in the wind, and he had an incredibly impish look to him. He jumped off the building to land next to her. Pounding his chest playfully, he replied, "Chillax, I'm not going to hurt myself. I'm made of pretty sturdy stuff." He looked at her, and his grey eyes went soft when he spoke.

"Yeah, like your heart, it's made of stone," Mina responded angrily.

Jared actually looked a little hurt at the barb. "Maybe, but that's because no one has ever taken the time to break through the stone and see that I do actually have one."

"Well, maybe it's because you are a jerk!" she snapped.

"Well, maybe I only pretend to be a jerk to keep from getting too close to people!" His tone slowly began to rise in pitch and volume.

"Then you must be lonely 'cause you seem to have yourself closed off from the world and protected just fine!" She turned angrily and pointed her finger, poking him hard in the chest.

"No! I don't have to protect myself from others. Only you!" He spoke the last two words barely above a whisper. He looked down at Mina's small finger jabbing him in the chest and frowned.

Mina didn't hear his whispered comment and sighed dramatically, dropping her finger. "Jared, you speak in riddles. Why can't you just spit it out? I don't have the time to figure out who you are, and what you want me to do or not do. Half the time, I think you're some kind of guardian angel my father sent to watch over me, and the other half I think you're the devil himself come to plague me about my curse."

"I'm not — " he began.

"I don't care anymore," she interrupted. "I've had a horrible night. I got into a fight with my best friend. No, my only friend. And my old boyfriend doesn't even remember me. Let's not even mention you. I've wasted enough time thinking you had died, and you weren't even hurt. I have plenty of reasons to be furious at you.

"Even tonight, I have no clue how you got here or why you're even here. Why *are* you here, Jared? Can you tell me who you are? Can you honestly look me in the eye and tell me the truth? One hundred percent truth, no lies, right now?"

Jared looked taken aback; his mouth opened in shock, and he was left speechless. Mina took his moment's hesitation for an answer.

"I thought so," she said sadly. She turned, pulled Nomer from the ledge, and went to stand by the fire escape to go back down. Her back was turned toward Jared, and her voice was stiff, hiding all the turmoil she felt deep inside. "I don't need people who can't be honest with me. I'm not a child that needs coddling. You know everything about me and my family. Things that no normal person could possibly know. I know you're not like me. I know that you're Fae. I've seen the things you can do."

"Mina, it's not like that... I want to — " Jared halted and clammed up.

Mina saw his resolve and his jaw clench in anger, in finality. He was almost going to tell her. She saw it. Then she saw the black cloud cover his face, and his expression froze. She knew then what she had to do. Walking down the steps to her window, she paused and looked up before entering her room and locking the window.

"I'm sorry, Jared. I wish you would tell me the truth. Because where there is truth, trust follows. And right now, at this very moment, I don't trust you."

CHAPTER 5

She didn't hear from Nan the whole weekend. Not once did the phone ring for Mina. It rang seven times for her mom and twice for her brother Charlie, who didn't even speak. Really, who would call a boy who was unable to talk? Apparently, Mikey, the kid in the next building over, had figured out that if no one was speaking after the phone was answered, it had to be her brother, and he usually asked if he could come over and play. One beep on the dial tone meant yes, two meant no. But still, it was a wonder that her brother was more popular than she was.

After her argument with Nan and her disappointing conversation with Jared, Mina became insanely grumpy and impossible to please. And everywhere she went she felt like she was being watched. It was like invisible static that hung in the air — a metaphysical bomb of fairy tale madness waiting to drop on her when she least expected it. She became jumpy and jittery, and knew that she was in the calm before a supernatural storm. She hadn't felt this much restless energy gathering around her since the Enchanted Dance, which meant whatever quest was coming was going to be a very dangerous one.

Mina was on edge at school on Monday. She began to suspect that everyone was in league with the Story against her.

Mrs. Porter was reading the school announcements in her gravelly voice, and her yellowed eyes never left the printed paper as she read. The woman was old-fashioned, high tech–disabled, tough as nails, and responsible for almost all of

Mina's tardy slips and detentions. Mina was only ever late to first period, and three tardies equaled a detention.

The cruel teacher was also known for trying to tempt students with last year's leftover candy corn, which she kept in a dish on her desk. Those actions alone had evil Fae written all over them. Mina knew without a teenage doubt that Mrs. Porter had to be an evil...something.

She was about to make a derogatory comment to Nan when she looked over and realized that Nan wasn't sitting in her usual spot next to her, but across the room next to Savannah White. Mina turned back to face the chalkboard and did her absolute best to not betray the emotions she was feeling. Yes, they had a spat, but she never in her lifetime would've thought her friend would abandon her for the enemy.

Wait! Mina's head whipped around unconsciously, and her eyes widened in disbelief. Why didn't she think of it sooner? Savannah White: Snow White. It was too ridiculous to believe, and only a dunce wouldn't have put the two together. How could the Story not try to manipulate Savannah into a tale? Now all Mina had to do was watch and wait.

Nothing interesting happened to Savannah White during first period. Mina's neck had a crick, and she'd acquired a splitting headache from trying to face forward while watching Savannah out of the corner of her eye for forty-five minutes. She dawdled and waited for Nan and Savannah to leave class before her so she could follow them.

Without sparing her friend a glance, Nan picked up her books and walked with Savannah down the hall. Mina slipped in behind them and observed carefully.

Nan smiled brightly as she flipped her hair in perfect imitation of Savannah. Her voice dripped honey. "So,

Savannah, my mom's boyfriend is letting us have a party at his cabin next weekend. You up for it?"

Savannah's smile faltered. "Cabin? As in woods, as in dirt?" It was obvious that she wasn't thrilled.

Nan's face only showed the mildest annoyance at Savannah's disdain, but she covered it well. "As in lake, boats, and boys."

Savannah perked up instantly. "Oh, I gotcha! Sounds fun! But for it to be a real party we need to make sure that we include…" They walked faster, and a student cut between them and Mina so she could no longer hear their party planning.

"Darn!" Mina muttered under her breath. She chewed on the inside of her cheek, debating whether to follow Savannah or head to her second-period class. Since nothing out of the ordinary seemed to be happening, Mina decided to head to class. She changed directions in the middle of the hall and ran right into the new girl with the spiky hair and Catholic school uniform.

"Watch it, gimp," the annoyed girl fumed. She pushed Mina out of the way and hurried toward a tall dark-haired boy leaning against a wall who was watching them both with interest.

Mina tried to call after her and apologize until she recognized the person the girl was making a beeline for — Jared. Mina stood stunned in the middle of the hallway as the cute girl caught up to Jared and leaned in close to him, really close. Closer than what was natural for just friends. Questions began to plague Mina. How did he know her? Did he have a girlfriend she didn't know about? How come he'd never mentioned her before?

She stood frozen in the middle of the hallway as student after student bumped into her. Some called out expletives for her to move. Jared leaned forward and whispered into the girl's short hair, in almost an intimate manner. She turned her small frame to him and tried to take a step closer. Jared shuffled, and it almost looked like he was giving her a hug. WHAT in the world was going on!

Mina's fingers dug painfully into her textbook, and she quickly put her head down and kept moving through the hall, hoping he didn't see her staring at him. How was this fair? Why could everyone, even Jared, carry on and have a normal life except for her? It wasn't until Mina walked into her biology classroom and saw a bunch of freshmen that she realized it was the wrong period and wrong class. Now she would have to turn around and walk past Jared and the girl *again*.

Her footsteps sounded immensely loud in the hallway, and she could feel her teeth grinding at the injustice that was high school. She wished she had her notebook of "Unaccomplishments and Epic Disasters" here with her because she would literally rip the whole thing to shreds. Her whole life was a disaster; nothing seemed to be going right. She didn't have a boyfriend, or a best friend, and she found herself insanely jealous of people she should be angry at. Whatever happened to her insanely boring, predictable, and clumsy life? It fell off the catwalk, that's what happened.

She found her destiny, or better yet, her destiny found her. How bad would it be really if she didn't complete any of the quests? Why couldn't the Fae run rampant through their world? No one had noticed it before. It couldn't be that detrimental if she didn't complete any quests, right? She could just ignore the Story.

Mina's spirits brightened as she sat down at her desk. Until she remembered the three bears and the missing homeless. She felt nauseous and felt even worse when she remembered who would be forced to complete the tasks if she didn't. Her younger, mute brother.

"Aaargh," Mina groaned and smacked her forehead into the desk, and decided to stare at the clock above Mrs. Colbert's head the whole period, counting the seconds until she could leave. All of her best-laid plans had failed. She thought and plotted and devised, but nothing fruitful came of it.

The morning passed without a single hint of magic, power, or segues of fairy tale specials. Nada. When lunch came, Nan still wasn't speaking to her, which was fine because it left it open for Mina to sit closer to Savannah's table and spy on her. It didn't exactly help when Nan sat right next to Savannah.

Mina watched Priscilla plait Savannah's hair to make a very intricate braid that included a blue ribbon down it. Mina gnawed on a carrot stick, and her eyes narrowed in hate. She couldn't believe it; she was sitting in the lunch room watching Brody's ex-girlfriend get her hair dolled up with ribbons. The carrot snapped off loudly in Mina's mouth, and she crunched it angrily. And not only that, but if the Story decided to use Savannah in a tale, Mina would have to rescue her butt.

"Ah, come on." Mina rolled her eyes as another cheerleader came over with her lunch tray and sat next to Nan, Savannah, and Pri. Everything seemed boring as usual, until Savannah asked for Pri's uneaten apple. Mina jumped up in eagerness. It was happening right now! Savannah thanked Pri, gently wiped the apple clean with her napkin, and slowly brought it to her pink-rouged lips.

Mina launched herself from the table next to Savannah's and quickly slapped the apple out of Savannah's hand. The apple flew across the floor and rolled into the black sneaker of a lone boy.

"OW! What did you do that for, Grimy!" Savannah screeched loudly, calling Mina that ugly nickname she hated. Savannah rubbed her hand where Mina had slapped it. A faint red mark was already appearing.

Mina hadn't prepared what she was going to say after she'd saved Savannah from being poisoned by the apple. Thinking fast wasn't her strong suit, nor was acting. Luckily, there was someone sitting close by who happened to be great at both.

"Oh, Savannah! Didn't you hear?" Nan answered nonchalantly. "There's been some sort of pesticide that has infected the out-of-state apple farms. Supposedly it hasn't reached the news yet, because only a few cases have been reported to area hospitals. But if you eat any apples from those farms, you could get really sick.

"I should know, my mom's boyfriend is a doctor, and since we don't know what farm that apple came from, it would be better if you just stayed away from all apples." Nan leaned forward and placed her head on the back of her hands, her eyes portraying all honesty.

Mina couldn't believe her good luck, She quickly moved away from Savannah's table, but not before she caught the smallest wink from Nan. She didn't understand the sudden change of heart from her friend or the reason behind her willingness to lie for her, but she was very glad.

She looked up and caught Jared's eye. He had watched the whole exchange, and he looked amused by Mina's actions. He pointed down at the apple that had come to rest against his shoe, the apple she had smacked out of Savannah's hand. He laughed as he reached down and picked up the apple. Mina frowned.

Dusting it off against his shirt, Jared took a bite out of it and chewed slowly, taunting her. Mina's mouth opened and closed in shock, and her level of frustration rose at his constant teasing. Jared laughed at her embarrassment. Mina retreated out of the lunchroom, his laughter following her.

~~~

Once school was over, Mina rushed toward her bike, only half eager to follow Savannah home. She knew that she would have to ride fast to catch up with a car. She couldn't wait until this quest was over and she could be done with her babysitting duties. She had just pulled the lock off her red Schwinn bike when a sleek black Mustang sped down the road toward the school. The driver was a showoff, driving fast, turning easily. Mina was slightly surprised when the car hit the brakes and stopped on a dime right in front of her. She could see her own reflection in the tinted windows of the high-end car and knew right then that she was in trouble.

If she knew what was good for her, she would've walked away, but curiosity got the best of her. She waited as the power windows lowered with only a small hum. Mina leaned down, expecting some sort of sport executive or celebrity VIP. She stepped back in disdain when she saw it was Jared.

He leaned across the passenger seat and whispered to Mina, "We need to talk."

Mina glanced warily over her shoulder and watched Savannah get into her blue convertible. Any minute now she would be gone. "No, I don't think we do," she answered out of the side of her mouth.

"YES, we do, and if you don't stop avoiding me, you are quickly going to be in over your head again."

"What do you mean, 'again'?" Mina argued.

"Can't you feel it? The storm brewing, the accumulation of power — the Story is building up toward another quest for you." At the word "quest" a small gust of wind blew against Mina, making her shiver.

"Yeah, I know. It's not my first rodeo. I'm way ahead of you, and I've already got it covered," she said, impatiently patting her jacket where she had tucked the Grimoire.

"Oh, you mean taking care of it like you did in the today in the lunchroom? You are way off track, and you obviously don't understand how these things work."

Mina gave Jared a disgusted look.

"Get in the car. I'll drive you home and we can talk."

"How do you know there's another quest coming?" She pointed her finger accusingly at him. "You haven't been very friendly or forthcoming with information yet."

"I'll explain later. Just get in." Jared reached forward and opened the door for her. Mina debated with herself. Jared might be the one person who could help her, and if he knew what was going on, then she needed his help. But, she told herself, if he lied to her, or if she thought she was in danger, she would run from him, and run fast. Somewhat happy with her plan, Mina nodded to Jared.

"What about my bike?" Mina pointed lamely toward her red bike, sitting crookedly in the bike rack.

"It will be back on your apartment landing before morning, but we need to talk and we NEED to talk soon." Jared was quickly becoming impatient.

"Just give me a minute." Mina turned and was going to put the lock back by the bike when Savannah rode by in her car, the top down, her blonde hair blowing in the wind. Mina felt her stomach sour at the prospect of spending more hours watching her, and was somewhat grateful for Jared's distraction.

Mina slid into the front seat, clicked her seatbelt, and looked toward the school's aquatic building. Coach Potts must have ended practice early, because Brody was walking toward his car, his blond hair still wet from the water. He was going to walk right in front of them. Mina's heart thudded in anticipation at seeing him. The car roared to life. Jared hit the gas and raced toward Brody angrily. Brody jumped back on the sidewalk, out of the way of the speeding car. He shot Jared a puzzled look.

CHAPTER 6

He was taking the long way home, or maybe just a different route. Either way, Mina was almost positive this was nowhere near where her family lived. She wasn't even sure if Jared knew where he was going. It was another ten minutes before she asked him the question that had been plaguing her.

"Where did you get the car?"

"Huh?"

"Don't play dumb. I know you have a black motorcycle. I even saw you crash it, and yet somehow you've been riding the same bike the last few weeks. I have never seen you drive a car before today, so where did you get this car?" Silence filled the air. When he wasn't forthcoming with an answer, she asked, "Did you steal it?"

"No!" he barked out angrily. "I did not steal it."

"Then where did you get it?" She crossed her arms indignantly and glared at him.

"It is none of your concern."

"Of course it's my concern. I need to know if I'm consorting with a criminal!"

"Mina, you know I'm not a criminal!"

"No, I don't. You've made certain that I know very little about you. For instance, who's the girl?" she asked.

Jared smirked. "What girl?" he answered innocently.

"The one you were practically making out with in the hallway at school," Mina exaggerated.

Jared snorted. "Jealous much?"

"No! I just wish you would tell me things," she answered pathetically.

"It's none of your business who I hang out with. It's safer that way."

Jared gripped the steering wheel and took the last turn a little too fast. She wasn't prepared and slammed her shoulder into the door painfully.

"No, what would be safer is if you would slow down," she argued, rubbing her shoulder.

Jared winced and decelerated the car. "Her name is Ever."

"Who is she?" Mina asked.

"Nobody you should worry about," he snapped.

It was the last straw. Mina was fed up with Jared.

"I've heard your pathetic excuses before. You sound like a broken record. You can't tell me, or you won't tell me!" She waved her fingers in the air at Jared. "Ooh, it's not safe if you tell me, it's taboo. Plus, you had no right to treat me like you did the last few weeks. You pretend that you don't even know me at school, and you won't tell me how you are alive and what happened after you crashed your bike. All of these things are important, and only when it's convenient for you do you want to talk to me. Well, I've had it. I want answers, and I want answers now."

"You won't like any of them," he stated simply.

"Then why ask me to get in the car?"

"Because I needed to speak with you privately."

"This is private. We are in a car *alone*."

"No, this isn't private enough. There are too many people. We need to be where no one can see us."

"Jared, you are really starting to scare me," Mina stated truthfully. Feelings of unease started to build.

He hit the steering wheel hard with the palm of his hand in frustration. Mina jumped. "That is exactly what I'm not trying to do." He looked at her with a worried expression etched across his face. "I'm trying to give you answers, and I don't want to scare you, but you are just so darn impatient."

Mina's body tensed up from the sudden mood change in the car. Everything had become extremely serious. "I don't care if I like the answers — I just want answers. I don't even know if I can trust you, if you are on my side," she stated softly.

Jared's jaw twitched, and she knew by his body language that she'd hit a nerve.

"Well, are you?"

"Am I what?" he answered a little too quickly.

"On my side?"

"Who says there has to be sides?"

"Of course there are sides. You are either with me or with the evil Fae who are always trying to kill me."

"Not all of us are always trying to kill you. It's just... complicated. Hey, there's an ice cream place up here. Do you want ice cream?"

Mina caught Jared's slip of the tongue and how he immediately tried to cover it. That misdirection might have fooled Nan, but it wasn't going to fool her. However, she did see something interesting next to the ice cream store.

"Yes, actually I do want ice cream," Mina lied.

Jared looked relieved and pulled into the vintage ice cream shop.

"Great, what do you want, double mint chip, vanilla, rocky road?" He pulled out his wallet and turned to her.

"Hmm, how about black raspberry chip?" She glanced out the window impatiently.

"Great, I'll be right back." He slipped out of the car and took the keys with him. Mina sat in the car and waited until

Jared had entered the store and stood in front of the menu board.

Quickly and quietly, she slipped open the car door, grabbed her backpack, and ducked around the building toward the bus stop. She had seen the transit bus a block away and ran toward the bus, pulling out her wallet. The bus had just pulled up, and Mina had her bus pass ready.

The driver was a burly elderly man with a name tag stating his name as Will and the words "Happy to Drive You" underneath it. Mina scanned her bus card and made her way to the back of the nearly empty bus. She stopped in the second to last row, tossed her backpack to the floor, and slouched down.

Two passengers got off the bus, and Mina didn't breathe until the bus closed its doors and started to pull way. She took a quick peek out the window toward Jared's car and the ice cream shop. There was no sign of Jared. He was probably still in the store.

Mina smirked, and a surge of adrenaline pumped through her when she realized she'd outwitted him. It had really freaked her out to be in the car with Jared and realize that he might not really be there to help her. His vagueness and stubbornness to answer questions proved it, along with the slip of the tongue. It might not have been obvious, but she had caught the slight change in his voice and his nervousness when she realized his mistake.

She couldn't believe how stupid she was. She knew Jared was Fae because he knew so much about her family and the Grimm curse. He had even used magic when he tried to train her and teach her. But his elusiveness and his refusal to tell her what she needed to know put him in the dangerous category. He wouldn't tell her who he was working for, who he was helping, and even if he was one of the good guys.

She knew that she probably shouldn't be angry at him, but he had ignored her. He also knew more about the Story than anyone she knew and still refused to tell her about it. That made him a traitor in her book. As long as she had the Grimoire, she didn't need Jared. It was the Grimoire, not Jared, that helped her battle Claire and LoneTree. She was the one who'd found the magical book that was supposed to help in time of great need. It was the one artifact that could help her complete the quests and banish the Fae back to their own plane. It's what had started it all.

Maybe that was what he was secretly after all along? Maybe he was trying to build her trust so he could steal the Grimoire for the Fae?

Mina leaned forward and hit her head against the bus seat. It was too much to ponder. She was going to need years to gain ground and finish the quests if she wasn't going to let her ancestors down.

The Brothers Grimm were the first to discover the existence of the Fae in the human world. Through research they discovered a way to cross to the Fae plane, and they confronted the ruling Fae, known as the Fates. They demanded that all Fae return to their own plane. The Fates agreed, if Jacob and Wilhelm could complete a list of quests. The Brothers agreed and traveled the world completing the innumerable quests. For every one they completed, it was logged into a magical book on the Fae plane.

When the Brothers began to struggle with their tasks, a kindhearted Fae split the magical book in two and gave one of the copies to the Brothers Grimm, to help them. This book was the Grimoire. It became the one thing that evened the playing field on the quests. And soon, everyone wanted the Grimoire; Fae on both sides wanted the book.

To make matters worse, the book on the Fae plane became self-aware and meddled with the Grimms' quests, forcing them to become part of the tales over and over again. For the more tales the Story collected, the more powerful it became, and the more deadly. For the book, known as the Story, wanted the Grimms to continue to live them out forever. There was one loophole the Brothers didn't cover. If they didn't complete the stories, then the next living Grimm would have the chance to complete them....all over again from the beginning.

It was a never-ending cycle of quests, stories, and tales to overcome. It became known as the Grimm curse, one which Mina's own father and uncle failed to complete and sacrificed their lives for. Now it was Mina's turn.

~~~

The bus let out a loud bang, and exhaust blew into the air as it pulled away from another stop. Mina woke up. She looked up from her seat and was taken aback by how much time must have passed. She must have fallen asleep. It was starting to get dark, and the bus was now completely empty. She didn't recognize any of the stops as being close to home and realized that she had ridden the bus line too far. They weren't even in the city but along back roads. She would have to get off and catch a different bus home. Mina pulled the cord to ring for the next stop.

"Excuse me! I'd like to get off!" Mina yelled from the back of the bus. The bus driver ignored her. His large form, which took up the whole driver's seat, looked larger than she remembered. She hesitantly stood up and made her way to the front of the bus.

"Sir, if you could pull over at the next stop, I would like to get off now." She gripped the pole by the seat.

The driver's body began to shake and shift as if he were trying to control his own form. There were loud slurping sounds and guttural growls coming from the driver. Scared that the driver was having a seizure, Mina reached for him and touched the back of his quivering uniform.

The driver reared up unexpectedly and turned toward her, revealing his true form. What she saw underneath the black bus cap was a large green head with grey eyes, large protruding teeth, and a bulbous nose. He was still wearing the striped driver's uniform and the same name tag. He opened his mouth and roared at Mina, exposing large bottom incisors.

"Behind the yellow line," he commanded in slow forceful words, barely recognizable because of the lisp he had from his protruding teeth.

Startled, she fell onto the floor of the moving bus as the ogre turned his head toward the road and continued driving.

CHAPTER 7

Holy buckets, she was on a bus being driven by an ogre! When the ogre made no more movement toward her, threatening or otherwise, she turned and hurried toward the rear exit door. There should be a safety feature where she could pull open the door, and, if necessary, jump. Mina gripped the rubber-lined door and pulled. It slowly slid open, exposing the rushing pavement beneath her. She looked toward the ogre bus driver. He still hadn't moved.

Could she do it? Could she really jump from a moving bus into the street? Would she die? Did it matter, if she might die anyway from being lunch for an ogre? No, she was going to have to jump for it. Sliding her backpack on, she closed her eyes and counted to three. One-two-three! She leapt into the air and felt a jolt on her back as something grabbed her forcefully from behind mid-jump.

Opening her eyes, Mina looked down and saw her feet dangling mere inches from the rushing pavement. She screamed in fright as she dropped farther, and her shoes dragged on the asphalt. Turning, she met the eyes of the angry ogre. He hauled her back onto the bus and forcefully pushed her into a bench seat, grunting at her to stay. He ambled back to the front of the bus and slid into the driver's seat again, just as the bus began to veer into a ditch. He gripped the wheel, grunted, and maneuvered it back onto the road.

The bus pulled off the main road and headed into the Mt. Adams National Forest. He took the bus down back roads and unmarked dirt paths. It was unbelievable that the bus even made it down the path. Moments later, the bus rolled to a stop. The ogre stood up and ambled toward her again, his large forearms bulging with muscles, which were overly long compared to his shorter legs.

Mina was prepared this time; she pulled out the Grimoire and held it up at the ogre, waiting for it to be sucked into the book. Nothing happened. The book was still a book. Mina screamed in fright as the Ogre reached for her jacket and lifted her up into the air. Suspending her in the air, the ogre growled and shook her as if trying to get her attention. Instead, she began to fight back by clawing and kicking, and the ogre just looked at her. In a moment of desperation, she hit the beast between the eyes with the corner of the notebook, and it flinched. He started to lower her to the ground, and she placed a well-aimed kick right between the Ogre's legs. He grunted and dropped her to the ground, leaning over in pain.

Mina scrambled frantically away, crawling on her knees toward the front of the bus. She was halfway to freedom when she realized she had dropped the Grimoire. Turning, she reached back to grab the notebook and then ran out the door into the night.

Breathing hard, she raced blindly through the dark woods, branches snapping loudly under her feet. She didn't waste precious time in trying to mask the noise she made. She heard a deafening roar split the forest from somewhere behind her. It was the ogre, and he was on the move after her. Her hands began to shake, and her chest burned from the exertion of running.

She tripped and fell forward into a ditch; the ground seemed to disappear from under her. Desperately, she grabbed at branches, rocks, anything to slow her descent as the incline became steeper. She thought it would taper out and her descent would slow, but instead she picked up speed. There was another sound of roaring, only this time softer, more constant, like water. Water!

She knew what it was and accidentally let out a scream of fear. She flailed, and her fingers found purchase on a large tree root. Her body left the embankment to hang in the air, and she began to tumble over a cliff. The roaring river passed some forty feet below her. Loud crashing and snarls came from above her, and Mina knew the ogre was closing in on her. She closed her eyes in fear.

Something brushed against her, and she looked up to see the ogre reaching down to seize her. Mina screamed again and scrambled out of reach of the large hands. The ogre roared angrily and tried to swipe at her back this time. She purposefully slid down the branch farther, closer to the water and away from the Ogre. At least she knew she would rather die from falling into the river, and possibly the rocks along it, instead of being eaten by an ogre. Isn't that what ogres in fairy tales did — eat people?

The ogre let out a quieter roar and became very still, as if trying to remain calm. Over the rushing water, she almost missed the sound of the ogre saying her name.

"Mina!"

She paused and looked at the ogre as he leaned down on his stomach, reaching for her. When he wasn't roaring at her, he didn't look as intimidating. Something magical began to happen as the ogre started to shrink. His features grew smaller and thinner, and became more human. The ogre, however, didn't take the form of the bus driver, but of a handsome dark-haired boy with grey eyes.

It was Jared. He reached for her arm, looking sick with worry. "I can't get to you in this form — you're too far away! Can you climb up farther?"

She should have felt relief at seeing her attacker take the form of Jared; instead she was furious at being duped.

"You jerk! How dare you!" Mina argued while refusing to climb closer to him. "If it wasn't for you I wouldn't be in this predicament."

"Stop arguing and get up here!" Jared was irritated at her again. "Now is not the time to berate me. There's plenty of time to do that later. Give me your hand."

Mina bit her lip and tried to pull her weight up the tree root so she could get closer to him, but her muscles had reached their limit. She tried to reach for Jared's hand, but she felt the root slip through her fingers, and then nothing but air. It was like being in a dream and falling in slow motion, except she didn't wake up when she hit the cold water.

CHAPTER 8

Cold ripped through her, and the shock of water made her lose the breath she was holding. It was dark, and she couldn't figure out which way was up. She tried to kick in the direction of the surface but couldn't find it. The current started to drag her away. She fought against it, and when she didn't think she could hold her breath any longer, she broke through the surface of the water. She gasped for breath. Her limbs felt heavy, and she couldn't get them to work. Slowly, and with great effort, she paddled for the riverbank. Finally, she dragged her body to the edge and pulled herself up the embankment.

She looked up river and saw something large, frantically diving down and up again. It was Jared in ogre form. He must have jumped in after her and was looking for her in the river. It was a comical sight, the giant ogre scrambling around in the water in an attempt at swimming. The awkwardness with which he fumbled in the water revealed to her that, in either form, Jared didn't know how to swim. The ogre had the better chance of surviving the fast-moving river than Jared. On any other night, it might have been touching to see him trying to rescue her, if she wasn't so annoyed with him.

As much as Mina wanted to laugh at the display of a frightened ogre, she couldn't forget his game and how he had tried to scare her on the bus. She decided that he could worry a little more. She moved down the river away from him and began to peel off her outer jacket, as it was making her cold.

Nevertheless, her movement caught the ogre's eye. He growled angrily and started stomping through the water toward the embankment. He was easily over nine feet tall and looked strong enough to bench-press a truck. But something about his current demeanor made him seem more childlike instead of deadly.

He was pouting. By the time he was within a few paces of her, the giant ogre had disappeared, to be replaced by a wet and tired Jared. He flung himself next to her on the ground.

"You could have shouted to me that you were okay, instead of sitting here all safe and sound, making me look like a fool."

"You are a fool," Mina replied as she tried to untie her wet shoelaces so she could get out of the wet socks.

"Point taken, but I thought you were dead."

"And I thought you were dead, so I think we're even." Mina's fingers were numb and like ice. She started to shake from the cold. She got one shoe off but was struggling with the second.

"Here, let me." Jared reached for her shoes to help her.

"Don't touch me!" she screeched, and hit him with her destroyed sneaker. Her teeth were chattering now, and Jared moved closer to her.

"I won't." He froze inches from her, his hands up in the air, as if he was waiting to be arrested.

"What happened to the bus driver?" Mina sniffed, using her sleeve to wipe pathetically at her nose.

"Uh, I tricked him into getting off a few stops ago, and I took his place." Jared slowly sat down on the ground across from her and folded his hands in his lap.

"And you can just do that? Change into his form and take his place?"

Jared looked at her and raised an eyebrow. "Yeah, *I* can — it's that easy."

"How did you find me? I mean, how did you know I was on the bus to begin with, and how did you...?" she trailed off, losing the ability to form coherent thoughts.

"You really think it was that hard to figure out you would ditch me as soon as we stopped? I saw it in your face. You're like an open book, and terrible at lying. As soon as I heard the car door close, I went out the back door of the shop and watched you get on the bus. It wasn't difficult to follow and take the place of the driver, with a little bit of Fae magic."

"Then why the show? Why the whole over-aggressive ogre thing?" Mina argued.

"I didn't think you would believe me if I told you that I'm not a bad guy. I mean look at me. I wanted to prove to you that I was the good guy. At first, I was going to scare you as the ogre and then run in to rescue you at the last minute as me. I was trying to prove a point that not all Fae are bad." He shoved his hands in his pockets and didn't make eye contact. "I wasn't planning on letting you see me change, but things got out of hand pretty fast, and I had no choice if I was going to try to save you."

"So you were going to try to scare me off as an ogre and then rescue me...from yourself?"

Jared looked down at his feet; he was still dripping wet and hadn't even attempted to try to dry himself off.

"Pretty much. I wanted you to trust me."

"By lying to me and deceiving me further?" She couldn't believe what she was hearing.

"Yeah, that was stupid. What can I say, I'm a guy, and we don't always think things through."

Mina rolled her eyes. "You can say that again, but this doesn't let you off the hook. All you've proved to me is that you're a prankster and a liar, and I still can't trust you."

"So I will have to prove it in a different way." Jared smiled crookedly.

"No more half-brain plans."

"Hey, my plans aren't always half-brain!"

Mina just looked at him squarely, and he chuckled. He picked up something off the embankment and handed it to her. It was the Grimoire.

"Oh, no! Now what do I do?" She immediately started to swing the notebook around to flick the water from it.

"It's fine — it can protect itself. Just ask it to re-form into another shape, it will dry."

Mina raised an eyebrow at Jared before envisioning the Grimoire into a much smaller, sturdier leather-bound book. A quick glow surrounded the book, and it shrank to fit her thought. "Wow, I don't know if I'll ever get used to that." She tucked it securely into her pocket.

"You'll have to get used to it. It's Fae magic," Jared said in a sour voice. He didn't seem too thrilled about it when he said it.

Sighing, she stood up and looked around, trying to find a way to get out. The river was on her left, and the cliff she'd fallen from didn't have an easy path up; it was pure shale. She looked across the river to the other side, and that cliff was even higher. They were going to have to walk along the river bed until they could find a shallower slope.

But then what? She had no clue where she was. She knew the national forest covered almost a thousand square miles, and they couldn't have possibly gone that far into the reserve, but what if they started walking the wrong way and ended up deeper into the woods? Granted, it was dark when Jared had pulled the bus over and she'd taken off running. She couldn't have run that far, right? Their best bet was to follow the river bed and hope it led them out.

Mina wrung out her socks and tucked them into her jacket. She put on her freezing-cold shoes and started to walk along the bank.

"Where are you going?" he asked.

"Home. I have to get out of here — my mom is going to be worried sick."

Jared jumped up quickly to follow along behind her as they walked. It was slow going with only the rising moon to guide their steps, and Mina frequently slipped and scraped her hands and knees. It probably would have been easier in the daylight, but the forest made her jump at every little sound. After a while, Jared took the lead, and they stopped often to listen for cars or other sounds of civilization, but all they could hear was the river.

Jared finally spoke up. "I think we're lost."

Mina didn't answer, and Jared turned to look at her. She was so tired she could barely stand. "You are done in." He turned to her and grabbed her shoulder, forcing her to turn to him.

She pulled away. "N-n-no. I have to get home." She was shivering uncontrollably.

"Mina! Your lips are blue! I'm so dense. I forgot how frail you humans are." Jared swatted away Mina's hands and pulled her over to an outcropping that jutted out from the cliff. It was a natural cave that didn't look big enough for one person, let alone two teenagers.

He pushed her inside and pressed his hands to the back of the cave wall. His hands began to glow, and she watched as the rock changed beneath his hands and moved back, making the cave bigger. When it was big enough for them to fit in it comfortably, but small enough to keep them warm, he switched to making a fire. He quickly dug a hole with a large rock, lined the hole with small kindling and a few sticks, and pulled out a Zippo lighter.

"What, you can't make fire?" Mina tried to joke, but she could barely get her mouth to form the words, and she was sure it came out in an unintelligible mumble. Mina didn't believe it would light, but was surprised when the spark produced a yellow-blue flame. Minutes later, Jared had a small fire going right outside the cave. Mina drew as close to it as she could, but her fingers were still frozen. She was so cold she actually considered putting her hands into the flames.

Jared crouched near her and began to rub her hands between his, trying to bring warmth back to them. His clothes were completely dry, and his body temperature was warmer than normal.

"Are you sick?" Mina asked. "You are so hot."

"No, I can make my body temperature rise to warm me." Jared unbuttoned his outer flannel and handed it to her. "Put this on."

Mina shook her head. "N-n-no."

"That wasn't a request! Here, I'll walk over there." Jared immediately walked a few paces toward the river, keeping his back to her.

Mina quickly took her shirt off and pulled on Jared's. It was completely dry already, unlike her shirt. It even smelled like him and was still warm with his body heat. When she was done, she laid out her shirt to dry on a bush. A few minutes later he walked back over to her.

"I think we should stay here until morning. We aren't making good time, and you need to get dry."

"But what about my mom?" she whined.

"There's nothing we can do now. She's probably already contacted the police, and they're looking for you."

"Oh, no! They're going to think that you kidnapped me!" Mina brought her hands up to her mouth in horror.

Jared just shrugged. "In a way, I kind of did."

"They won't know where to look!"

"I'm sorry, Mina. This is my fault," he said solemnly.

"Yes, Jared. It is." A few seconds later her stomach growled noisily, and Jared started laughing.

"Holy cow! Did you hear that?" he blurted out.

Mina punched Jared in the arm. "I'm hungry, which happens to be your fault, too." Ignoring him, she crawled into the small cave and tried to curl in a ball to sleep.

"Hey, is there room for me?" Jared looked into the cave expectantly.

"NO!" Mina growled at him. "Don't even think about it. And just because you got us into this, you can keep watch and tell me if you see anything. "

"Fine," Jared said, and leaned against the outer wall of the cave.

A few moments of silence passed, and Mina was almost asleep when she heard Jared speaking out loud in a droning voice. "I'm keeping watch, and I *see* the river. I *see* the moon rise over the trees. I *see* that the forest looks really, really creepy right now. I bet you there is some sort of killer vampire turtle slowly crawling toward us out of the woods. Yep, I can almost hear its little turtle-y steps inching closer to us."

"Jared?"

Mina had no idea where Jared's sense of humor suddenly came from, but it seemed to pour out of him in the most annoying boy fashion. Something about being outdoors and away from people brought out a different side of him. He didn't seem so surly and angry. Maybe it was because something had changed between them, or he didn't feel like he was hiding from her anymore. He was finally free to be himself. Mina would bet anything that there still were loads of things he wasn't telling her…but it was a start.

"Yeah?" he answered a little too brightly.

"Are you going to shut up?"

"Nope," he answered back. She could hear the grin in his voice.

"Will you shut up if I said please?"

"Probably not!" He chuckled. He was enjoying teasing her.

"Fine, then you can sleep in the cave if you promise me that nothing is going to *eat us* during the night."

"I promise that if something comes to harm us during the night, I will *eat it* instead." Jared crawled into the small cave, being careful to not touch her. He turned on his side and faced away from her. Mina mirrored the action. She watched the dying fire cast shadows on the cave wall.

All of a sudden, Mina couldn't sleep with Jared so close to her. For some reason, questions kept plaguing her, and they were ones she was pretty sure he wouldn't answer. She shivered again from the cold, as her pants were still wet. But you could bet to high heaven they were staying on.

"So how come you never told me you're an ogre?" she asked quietly, her finger tracing circles on the ground.

"You weren't ready," he stated simply.

"And what made you decide to tell me now?"

"I was tired of you always being angry with me because there are some *things* that I can't tell you. And, in a way, I wanted you to know. You also have to remember that I'm not gonna win homecoming king in my Fae form." There was something in his voice that sounded vulnerable. Gone was the tough biker Jared, replaced by a young teenage boy who just wanted to be liked, to fit in. But she could tell he was still withholding something.

"So how come the Grimoire didn't work on you? Isn't it supposed to protect me when I'm in trouble?"

"It won't work on me." Jared sighed loudly, trying to sound annoyed, like he was the one who was almost asleep.

"Why not?" Mina asked.

"'Cause I'm cool like that." He laughed.

Mina snorted. "Really? You're going to evade the question? I actually thought that you were going to be truthful with me."

"Mina, I don't know what to tell you, other than the Grimoire can't harm me. Call it ogre power if you must."

She pondered what he said for a moment before asking, "It can't or won't?"

"Both…neither. I don't know what you are trying to get at."

Mina worried at her bottom lip before speaking again. This time it came out in a whisper. "I just need to know that the Grimoire is still going to protect me. I want to know that, next time, it is going to work. I don't know what my father did wrong, but the Grimoire wasn't able to help him, and he died during one of these stupid godforsaken quests.

"Today, when I opened the book and tried to use it on you, it didn't work. I panicked and really believed I was going to die, like my father."

"Oh…" Jared became quiet. "You wished I would've gotten sucked into the book then. Boy, you really must not like me!"

Mina was annoyed. "I didn't know it was you, remember! And yes, truthfully, like right now, I almost wish the book would suck you into it."

Jared made a noise that sounded like laughter. When she became quiet, he apologized. "I'm sorry, I can tell this is really bothering you."

"Yes, it is. The Grimoire came to my Uncle Jack, and he died. My father had it and became obsessed with ending the curse on our family. Even with the help of the Grimoire, he wasn't strong enough. I just…" Mina became choked up. "I thought today was it. The end…and I'm not ready to die."

~ ~ ~

Jared could hear her crying softly, and guilt like he had never felt before overcame him. "Mina," Jared said softly, turning toward her in the cave; he leaned up on one elbow to look at her. "Mina, look at me." She turned to look at him; her brown eyes appeared even larger with tears in them. "It will work next time. I promise."

Her voice sounded small, like a child's. "How can you be sure?"

For once in his life he really wished he could believe his own words as he tried to comfort her. "I'm just sure."

She nodded halfheartedly and turned back to looking at the wall. A few minutes later, she had cried herself to sleep. He watched her sleep, and when she continued to shiver, he slid closer to her and wrapped his arms around her, spooning her while she slept. He knew that she would never allow this while she was awake, but it was the only comfort he could give her. He breathed in her hair. Even after the dunk in the river, she still smelled faintly of strawberries.

He had to be better at shielding himself from her. She was breaking down his walls and leaving him vulnerable. He knew that he couldn't always protect her, that one day he would be commanded to leave her side. He just hoped, beyond hope, that those commands would never come. But more than that, he was scared that she was being tracked.

It was one of the reasons he'd brought her out here, to hide her scent trail from that which hunts the Grimms. But he didn't think he could ever tell her how her ancestors really died. It was easier to let her believe it was the Grimoire's fault. Sometimes people were better off not knowing about the things that went bump in the night.

CHAPTER 9

Mina dreamed of ogres. Being chased by ogres, eaten by ogres, and finally caught and smothered by an ogre. She dreamed that she was wrapped in its arms and it was hugging her to death. When she awoke, she was in the cave alone.

Sounds of a crackling fire drew her attention to the cave opening. Jared was cleaning a fish, and there was one already cooking over the fire.

"How did you catch those?"

"I was a Boy Scout." Jared held up two fingers in imitation of a Boy Scout salute.

"I highly doubt that." Mina laughed. "For some reason, I don't think you would have the patience to sit through all of those club meetings. Besides, if you were a Boy Scout, we would already be out of here."

"You're right. I'm not. I was too much of a troublemaker to be a Boy Scout. Let's just say I'm a bit of an ogre achiever and my good looks helped get you breakfast."

"Hey, I'm not going to question food as long as it ends up in my belly," Mina remarked.

Jared turned the fish over one more time before serving it up to Mina on a large piece of bark. The fish was juicy, hot, and lacked seasoning, but she was too hungry to care. She burned her tongue in her impatience to eat.

When they had both eaten their fill and drank enough of the cold river water, it was time to go. Jared kicked dirt over their ashes and put out the rest of their fire. It wasn't a warm day; in fact, it was still very chilly and overcast. The gloominess was depressing and made their trek even more miserable.

"So, tell me more about the quests. You said that you knew one was coming — how is that?" Mina asked quietly.

"Well, because I'm Fae and I can feel the buildup of power, and you should be able to as well. It's like a tidal wave that pulls back and builds. All you get is a glimpse of small waves starting to form, followed by stillness and then the storm."

Mina nodded her head. "I've felt it, and I think I've always been able to feel it. For me it starts as a tingling sensation throughout my body, or like being covered in static cling. It's been happening ever since my dad died. There was always this feeling of someone watching me."

Jared glowered angrily at the news and kicked at a rock as they walked. "Well, yes, that probably would've been the Story you were feeling. The Fae aren't without some pity. It probably was waiting, checking up on you, and biding its time until all of the perfect elements were in place. It has learned to wait until the Grimms have gotten older before unleashing a quest on them. The young ones aren't very fun."

Mina gasped out loud and turned to stare at him in shock. "Do you mean that you've made children try to solve the quests? That is horrible! I almost didn't survive it!"

"Wait, not me! I didn't make children do anything. Like I said, this was long ago and is one of the reasons the Story decided to wait before assigning another quest. Many of the Grimm children did overcome the quests, but most didn't. A lot of the Fae didn't like that the Story started on the Grimms at such a young age. Remember there are quite a few factions in our world that are pro-human. So the Story started waiting until the next Grimm came of age."

"And what is the right age?" Mina asked angrily.

"Sixteen."

"But I was still fifteen when all this started. It was my birthday, my sixteenth birthday, that I beat the Hansel and Gretel and Red Riding Hood tales!"

"What can I say — you're kind of a remarkable girl. You happened to catch the Story's attention a little early." He shrugged and stuffed his hands into his jeans.

Heat rushed to her cheeks at the compliment. Mina stopped to rest by crawling on top of a large river boulder. Slowly, she removed her shoes and shook them upside down, dislodging a rock that had maneuvered its way in and was stabbing her foot. It hadn't gotten any warmer, but Mina was tired and needed to rest.

Jared was leaning against a nearby tree with his eyes closed, waiting patiently for her. The sound of the river was soothing, and if Mina weren't here under these conditions and with her present company, she probably would've enjoyed the trip a whole lot more. But as it was right now, this was agony.

With his eyes still closed, Jared spoke up. "Did you know that the first Hansel and Gretel were actually Fae, and it was the old woman who was a Grimm?"

"What are you talking about? That doesn't sound right."

"This is where it can get a little confusing, and quite funny. In the very first quest, Hansel and Gretel were thieves and murders, like, um, Bonnie and Clyde. But because Hansel and Gretel were Kitskin, child-like Fae that never grow old in appearance, no one ever suspected them. Your namesakes figured it out.

"The Kitskin never robbed the same house twice, and it was usually only the elderly they robbed. It was Wilhelm who thought of a plan to catch them. He had Jacob dress like an old woman and lure the Fae to his front door with the offer of sweets."

Mina started to laugh as she pictured her family member trying to cross-dress.

Jared opened one eye, and his dark eyebrow arched high in indignation. He refused to continue until she had decided to stop interrupting him.

"Sorry," Mina mumbled and folded her elbows over her knees and leaned her chin on her forearms. It was as good a position as any to hear the whole story.

"Hansel and Gretel looked inside and were tempted by all the jewelry and money the Grimms happened to have laid out on the table. Later that night, Hansel and Gretel snuck back into the house to kill them and make off with the loot, but instead they were trapped by the Brothers in a magical cage and oven, thanks to the Grimoire." He sounded smug.

"It sounds so easy when you tell it that way. Way easier than my own Hansel and Gretel encounter." Mina lifted her head, and when she saw Jared's perturbed look, she covered her mouth with her hand and shrugged.

"Yes, they do sound pretty easy, but remember, not every quest can be completed. They aren't all deadly quests, and you do get a chance to retry them."

Her hand shot straight up into the air like an eager student in class. Jared waited a full three seconds before calling on her.

"Okay, now you can ask a question." He pointed at her with a stray branch he had picked up from the ground.

"So what about Claire?"

"Claire was becoming a loose end and dangerous. Unfortunately, because this is the human world, the Fae don't have to answer to anyone. So the Story will try to push these particular Fae into your path, hoping you will eliminate them for the Fates."

"So I'm like the Ghostbuster for the bad Fae that your King and Queen can't control anymore. They purposely send them my way and hope that I will trap them in the Grimoire."

Jared glared at her for not raising her hand. Mina smiled apologetically.

"Yeah, it's kind of a win-win. The Grimms need adversaries, and the Fae need a few less...um, bad guys. There has to be an equal balance. That's why so many of them want the Grimoire, because with it they, too, can trap their enemies within its pages. There are also a few other perks or rumors about the Grimoire that make them want it...but none of them are true," he finished quickly, a little too quickly.

Her hand shot into the air again. Jared nodded again impatiently at her.

"So what's to keep me from ignoring the quests and running away and living to a ripe old age? I mean, if I don't complete them, then the gate will never be shut and the Fae will be free to roam both worlds. It's a win-win for me, right? Life and life."

Jared stared at the stick in his hands before snapping the thin wood into pieces. He broke them again and again before turning and chucking them angrily into the bushes. Startled birds took off into the sky. Turning, breathing hard, he looked at her, his eyes sad.

"That is where the Story comes in. A promise is a promise, and if a Grimm doesn't complete the quests in a timely matter, then the Story begins to set up the quests and forces the Grimm into it. This time without giving them a choice in which quest, or a how it plays out. Remember when I told you that the Story is alive with power? Well, it's more than that. It thinks, breathes, and manipulates you like a pawn on a chessboard. But even a pawn is strong enough to take out a Queen. So think about that, will you, before you try to run from your destiny."

He was right; there was a lot to think about. Tired, sore, and a little defeated, Mina stepped down off the boulder, and they continued their long trek. A few hours later, Jared wanted to stop and try to catch them some lunch, but Mina wanted to press on.

Finally, the cliff tapered off and the steep shale was replaced by dirt and trees. Mina and Jared were finally able to climb the steep embankment and get away from the river. In her head, Mina pictured that if she could just get out of the valley with the river that civilization had to be minutes away. She was wrong. They *had* been walking in the wrong direction, and there were moss-covered trees for miles around. Every direction she turned looked the same.

"Now what?" Mina groaned. Her feet were killing her; it had started to rain slightly, and she was starving. She truly believed that they were heading in the right direction, but once they got out of the riverbed, she realized her mistake.

"I don't think I can do this anymore." She was so crushed by her discovery she actually turned to Jared for answers. But her simple turn became a fall when her shoe slipped on the wet leaves, and she started to pitch backward down the steep embankment they had just climbed.

Jared lunged toward Mina and caught her shoulder, but her awkwardness and flailing arms caused them both to tumble backward down the embankment toward the hard riverbed once again. Thinking quick, Jared twisted in midair so he took the brunt of their fall.

One minute she was sliding on the rocks, pitching backward, and the next she was wrapped in Jared's arms at the bottom of the embankment, warm and protected. At a loss for words and unwilling to move first, she just lay there face to face with him, intensely aware of how close they were and how tightly he was holding her.

She had always known that Jared was attractive. His dark hair, strong jaw, and grey eyes made him irresistible, but Mina could never get past his ugly attitude. His pride, arrogance, and the disdain he usually seemed to carry just for her helped keep her in check.

His eyes were closed, and she could make out each individual eyelash. His lips were slightly parted as he breathed slowly, trying to regain his breath from the fall. The faint rain splattered his cheek, and in this moment, everything else forgotten. Jared was breathtaking.

She should move, lean back and pull away, but she didn't, couldn't, mostly because his arms were wrapped around her, and he didn't seem to be in any hurry to release that hold.

He still hadn't opened his eyes. Mina almost thought maybe he was unconscious, but she knew that to be a lie, because her hand was resting across his chest, and the longer she stared at his face, the faster her heart raced…and Jared's heart was racing faster.

Finally, he swallowed and opened his eyes, and she almost drowned in the raw emotions she saw in them. He was going to kiss her! She gasped when she realized his intent, and she wished she hadn't, because he misunderstood her anticipation for rejection. He immediately went cold. His jaw tightened, and he looked hurt. He let go of her, and she felt a little disappointed when he reached up toward her face and pulled a stick out of her hair.

"Next time, try not to take the whole forest with you when you fall." He smiled slowly, but the smile never reached his eyes. He pulled another twig from her hair and handed both of them to her. "For your Christmas tree next year," he joked.

She scrambled away from Jared and instantly felt the loss of his warmth; it was so much warmer being snuggled up next to him. Her cheeks burned with embarrassment, but thankfully he didn't notice.

He sat up slowly but remained on the ground. He stared at his hands for a moment before looking at her. He looked solemn and determined. Whatever he was about to say, she knew she wasn't going to like it.

Large crashing from the nearby bushes interrupted them, and they both looked up in alarm. There was no time to run or scream before a large beast appeared in front of them. Mina froze as the black bear towered over her. All she could see were eyes and teeth as it moved in for the kill.

Mina screamed.

CHAPTER 10

The black bear lunged for Mina, swiping at her with its powerful paws, trying to knock her back. Jared shifted into his ogre form and dove between them, taking the force of the bear's blow and getting slashed across his forearm in turn. The bear was undeterred at the sight of the larger ogre and became even further enraged. Ignoring Mina, it focused its attack on the new, larger threat.

Jared rushed forward into the bear's clutches and physically began to push and wrestle the bear away from Mina, who was paralyzed with fear. Swipe after swipe, the bear used his most powerful weapons, his paws, to try to dislodge Jared, but he was too close for those paws to do much damage. Unfortunately, that only put him closer to the bear's second strongest weapon, his teeth.

Mina cried out when the bear twisted its head and bit down on Jared's left shoulder. He roared in pain and punched the bear in the snout, causing the bear to release its painful grip. Jared grunted and wrestled with the bear, and was able to grab it around the middle to lift it high in the air above his head. He turned, took three large steps, and tossed the bear into the river. The bear went under, broke the surface, and swam toward them, this time keeping a greater distance when it circled them threateningly again.

The bear rose to its hind legs and roared at them. Jared moved toward the bear and roared back in challenge. Startled and a little unsure, the bear dropped and ambled off into the thicket.

Jared stayed in ogre form until the bear had disappeared, only changing back when he was sure they were safe. Mina watched him in fascination as his skin took on a more normal pink hue and his features shrank and disappeared, until he stood before her, bleeding, spent, and fully human.

His head drooped in fatigue, but he looked up at her and smiled wanly before collapsing to his knees in pain. Mina rushed to his side and ripped open his T-shirt to see the damage to his shoulder. It was bloody and messy, but he didn't look to have broken any bones.

"I'm fine. It looks worse than it feels," he lied terribly.

"Oh, Jared, you could have been killed. We have to get out of here. More bears could come back, and we don't want to be here." She tore off a strip of her shirt, and ran back to the water and started to clean the wound.

"We will be fine as long as we don't make any sudden moves in the direction of that thicket." He sat down on the ground and let Mina tend to the bite on his shoulder and the cut along his arm. He closed his eyes and nodded toward the place where the bear had both appeared and disappeared.

"How can you be sure?" Mina asked hesitantly. It was too much like being attacked by the cannibalistic bears, but the Grimoire wouldn't work in this real situation.

"It was our fault. We startled a mother and her cubs when we fell down the embankment. The cubs were hiding in the thicket the whole time. She was just being a good mom." He hissed in pain when she pressed too hard against the wound.

Mina glanced over at the thicket and was barely able to see the retreating form of the mother black bear and two rambunctious cubs bumbling after her.

Jared rested for a few moments with his eyes closed before he took a closer look at his wounds. Slowly, he got up and began to look around the base of the tree trunks. Mina asked what he was doing, and he explained that he was looking for Eros moss, a plain-looking tree moss that the Fae loved for numbing pain. It was easy to find, since the moss grew everywhere. He got Mina to apply it and bandage his wound. Satisfied, he motioned for them to continue their journey.

Mina kept close to Jared, worried that he might collapse or fall down from fatigue. But the Eros moss seemed to be doing its job, because Jared never slowed his pace, but picked it up. It actually looked like he was the one becoming impatient with her slowness.

"Do you like to climb trees?" he asked.

Mina looked at the huge pine tree they stopped next to apprehensively. "Not really, but I can try." She began to scale the tree, but about fifteen feet up, her natural clumsiness got the best of her, and she slipped and sliced her arm on a broken branch. Pain laced up her arm, and she cried out.

"Stay there — I'm coming up," Jared yelled up at her.

"No, I got this!" She knew he wasn't in any condition to climb a tree. Gritting her teeth, she slowly ascended to the top. She spent a few minutes looking around at the surrounding landscape. What she saw was discouraging. A few agonizing minutes later she was back on the ground next to a perplexed Jared.

"So what did you see?" he asked carefully.

"A whole lot of trees," she grumbled under her breath.

"Ah," he intoned casually. "Well, let's go this way." He pointed left.

"How do you know where to go?" She looked around and back up at the sky, confused.

"Because I know we need to go east," Jared answered.

"But it's overcast and cloudy, and we can't even see the sun. How do you know which way is east?" Mina waved her arms and pointed at the grey sky. The sky took that moment to start to rain down on them. "See!"

"Because the moss grows on the north side of trees, so as long as you head this way, you'll get out."

Mina stopped and stared at Jared in disbelief. "If you knew that already, why in the world did you have me climb the tree?"

Jared looked at her, his eyes widening in innocence. "I didn't ask you to climb the tree. I knew which way we were heading. I just asked you if you liked to climb trees in an attempt to start a conversation. You were the one who wanted to try to climb the stupid tree."

"I did not," Mina tried to argue, but realized that she was the one at fault.

They trudged through the slight drizzle, and soon all of her clothes were once again soaked. Another hour in, and she started to shiver and sneeze. If they didn't get out of this soon, they were going to catch pneumonia.

"How much longer?" she asked.

"Hey, how am I supposed to know?" He was becoming cross.

"Well, can't you do any magic to make it go faster?" Mina whined. The pain in her arm was starting to sting and make her more irritated than she already was.

"What, do you think I'm some kind of genie in a bottle that can grant you three wishes?" Jared fumed angrily.

"Are you really that selfish that you can't help us out? If you can get us out of here, then you should," Mina yelled back. "It's your fault that we're lost in the woods to begin with, so don't you think you should try and get us out?"

"I'm not your beck-and-call boy. You don't tell me what to do!" Whatever she'd said really set Jared off, because he turned his back on her, and the happy-go-lucky Jared from last night and this morning was gone, to be replaced by the surly one she used to know.

His footsteps became longer and faster, and Mina had to start running to catch up with him. "Look, I'm sorry. I shouldn't have said what I did. I didn't know it was going to make you so angry. So you will have to forgive me if I'm not my most congenial self at the moment. I'm tired and sore, and I know that my mother is probably worried sick and desperate to hear from me. I just want to get home to my family, and I will do almost anything to get there. Do you have any idea what that's like?"

He stopped when they came to a small cliff overlooking the forest below. He stood there still as a statue and waited for Mina to catch up to him.

"Yes, I do know what it is like to want to desperately go home." He turned to look at her, and his face was detached, his grey eyes that moments ago were crinkled in laughter—void.

"Then why don't you just disappear and go back home to the Fae plane?"

"Because I am unable to cross over. I'm stuck here." He turned his back to her.

"But why? What happened?" Mina asked quietly.

"It's none of your business," he answered heatedly. He turned and stared back out across the forest as if he was searching for something. He raised his head and sniffed the air; his shoulders stiffened in anger. "I have a confession to make," he growled.

Mina felt her mouth grow dry with dread, and she swallowed nervously.

Jared cleared his throat. "I did this on purpose."

"What do you mean, you did this on purpose?" She couldn't even fathom what he was referring to: the bus ride, tricking her — there were endless possibilities.

"I purposely brought you out to the middle of the forest to make sure you got lost."

She went cold at his words. There was no way he was serious after saving her from a fall and protecting her from an angry black bear. He had to be joking. He wasn't.

"I have to leave you here." He looked at her, his eyes dark and angry. She went still.

"Please, tell me you aren't seriously going to abandon me." She stood still next to him, pleading with her voice, letting all her fear and insecurities pour out.

"I have to. Something bad is coming, and I need rest. Otherwise, I won't be able to help you," Jared whispered. There was a catch in his voice. "Just promise me you'll be careful and stay on the path."

"Path? What path?" Tears of pain and frustration burned at the corner of her eyes. She blinked them away, and when she opened her eyes, Jared was gone.

She spun in a circle to look for him, but he had vanished. There was no evidence of footsteps, sounds, or bushes being disturbed. He just disappeared. Mina called his name, but no one answered except for the echo of her voice off the valley. Dejected and alone, she sat down in the dirt and rain and stared out over the forest.

How could she have ever trusted him? He was, she decided, the absolutely worst kind of Fae. She didn't think that they were capable of disappearing like that, but obviously they did it, and did it a lot. He probably was in league with the Story against her. He was being the evil stepparent figure leading her out into the forest and abandoning her.

She turned to look angrily across the forest and saw what Jared had seen. A path. It seemed to be a few miles off. But if she got moving, she could get there by nightfall.

She took Jared's moss advice, hoping it was accurate, and started walking in an easterly route. It took her two hours to reach the dirt access road.

The dirt road came to a fork, and Mina wasn't sure which one to take. They both traveled along somewhat the same route. She chose the path that went right. After another hour, she was sure she'd chosen the wrong path. But wasn't it better to keep going on the same path instead of backtracking?

Mina's feet were dragging, and she slipped on a muddy rock and twisted her ankle. Crying out in pain, she crumpled to the ground. Biting her lip, she tried to stand up and continue walking, but as soon as she put weight on her ankle, she fell to the ground again. Tears of pain and frustration rained down Mina's face as she half crawled, half dragged herself along the road.

If she'd been one to curse, she knew she'd be calling Jared all kinds of nasty names. But instead she envisioned all the terrible things she was going to do to him if he ever dared to show his face to her again.

A crack of thunder made Mina jump, and she looked up as the clouds turned ugly and let out their fury in a downpour of rain. Wasn't this just like her luck?

She half dragged, half crawled her way to the side of the road to take shelter under a tree. Her skin felt like ice, but her hatred of Jared kept her warm. Just when she was about to give up hope of ever being found, a light in the distance pierced the darkness.

She tried to yell, but her voice felt hoarse. The light grew bigger, drew closer, and became two lights. They were headlights. Mina used the tree for support and pulled herself up into a standing position so she could be better seen from the road. She could just make out a black Jeep coming her way. Mina began calling out and waving her hands through the darkness and rain, hoping the car wouldn't drive past her. It wasn't slowing down.

Panicking, Mina began hopping on one leg toward the road in an attempt to intercept the moving car. Just when she was almost there, she slipped and fell into the road, right in the direct path of the speeding vehicle. Looking up, she could see her death coming as the driver of the Jeep hit the brakes. It spun out of control in the mud and began to fishtail, heading right for her!

CHAPTER 11

Crack! A large tree fell on the road in between Mina and the out-of-control Jeep. Mina screamed as the branches pinned her to the ground. She gritted her teeth as the Jeep spun sideways into the downed tree, sending the tree and Mina sliding down the road in the mud. Thankfully, the trunk of the tree took the force of the car's impact. The vehicle had sideswiped the large tree and looked to be in worse condition than the evergreen.

She heard a car door slam.

"Hello! Are you there?"

"I'm here!" Mina tried to yell back through the storm. She could barely see, as broken branches and pine needles covered most of her body. She held up her hand in the air, and someone began to clear branches off her body. Lying there in the mud, during a storm, Mina couldn't help but be thankful that she was alive. She really thought she was a goner. Strong hands gripped her and helped pull her to a sitting position.

"Are you hurt anywhere?" the man asked. He looked shaken from the accident, but otherwise fine.

"My ankle — I twisted it," Mina answered.

The man stopped and stilled. "What's your name?" he asked.

Mina looked closely at her rescuer. He was of medium build, with olive-toned skin and brown eyes and slightly curly hair. She didn't recognize him. But a whisper of a voice told her to lie and do it well. "Nan Taylor."

She watched as he ran back to the Jeep and called in to someone on his C.B. radio. She couldn't hear the answer coming from the radio, but it was obvious that he was out searching for someone. Help had come. But what kind?

The man came back to Mina and helped pull her to her feet, being careful of her injured leg. He introduced himself as Karl, and helped Mina wobble to his car. He grabbed a rain poncho and flashlight from the back of the vehicle and walked around it, checking under the hood and under the rear of the vehicle.

Mina used the time to look around at the inside of the all-terrain vehicle, which seemed to belong to a survivalist. She could see a tent, coolers, and various large black bags. A feeling of unease came over her at the sight of the barrel of a gun sticking out of a bag, but Mina decided to push the feelings aside. After all, this man did save her, and he didn't look to be carrying a weapon actually on him. Maybe he was a hunter and this was the off season. After a few minutes, he jumped into the car and clicked off the flashlight.

"I've got good news and bad news. The engine is fine, but we have a broken rear wheel axle, so we won't be going anywhere fast, but at least we'll be dry until help arrives."

"Is help coming?" Mina asked hopefully. Her whole body was shaking, partially from shock and partly from cold.

"We will be fine." Karl turned the key in the ignition and flipped the heaters on full blast. He reached into the back seat and pulled out a foil blanket that looked too thin to do any good. "Here, it's a thermal blanket — it will use your own body heat to keep you warm. It looks like you've been out there a while." He switched blankets with Mina and then threw the wool one on top of her lap.

Warmth slowly started to creep into her hands, but her feet and toes still felt frozen to the bone. "You sure are prepared for everything," Mina stuttered out. She looked at the car radio, and the time read 10:30 p.m. Did it really take her all day to make it across the valley?

Karl pulled out a granola bar and a silver thermos, handing the granola bar to Mina. Her hands were shaking, and she gave up trying to open the package. She was so tired; all she wanted to do was sleep. She leaned against the window pane and watched the rain splatter against the glass, gather into large pools, and then slide down.

He got the thermos open and poured a cupful of coffee into the lid, handing it to her. Mina sipped the coffee and tried to listen to what Karl was saying. Her eyes were becoming increasingly heavy, and it was hard to concentrate in the warm vehicle.

"You must be the luckiest girl in the world. You know that, don't you?" His lips pressed together. He studied her under heavy-lidded eyes.

Mina wasn't so sure it was luck. She made sure to take a good look at the trunk of the tree as Karl helped her into the car. The tree wasn't hit by lighting. There was no evidence of charring or it being cracked or split. The hundred-foot tree was uprooted, but most of the tree's roots were still buried deep in the ground. Something of extreme force had hit the tree, causing it to fall into the road. Mina was almost positive it was Jared, but why?

The car felt like it was on fire and burning her up. She tried to move her hand toward the heater to turn it down, but Karl mistook her actions for wanting more heat. He turned the knob up, and Mina's hand felt heavy and dropped uselessly on her lap. She was having problems even controlling her own limbs. The intense heat emanating from the car's heaters made it almost impossible for her to breathe and she started to shiver again, but this time from a fever.

She heard Karl speak to her, but she couldn't respond, couldn't move. She heard a chuckle, and felt his hand touch her cheek and forehead. She felt the seat move and heard the sound of something being opened in the back seat. She passed out and awoke a few moments later to the sound of a siren.

Karl cursed out loud and picked up the radio again. He mumbled something into it about being "too late to be sure."

Another vehicle pulled up beside them. More people piled out of the other vehicle. Her door opened, and she was moving through the air.

She opened her eyes to see she had been moved onto a stretcher and someone was taking her blood pressure. She blinked, or at least she thought she did, and the next time she opened her eyes, she squinted in pain because she was in a hospital. Doctors, nurses, and a familiar voice spoke in hushed tones. Her fever raged on most of the night and into the next day. Sometime the next night it broke.

"Mom?" Mina said quietly, and a hand encompassed her own and squeezed gently. She heard her mother's voice whisper to her that she was going to be all right. Mina relaxed and drifted back to sleep.

~~~

Something was touching her nose! Mina's eyes flew open to stare at an offending feather assailing her face. Her eyes followed the large white goose feather to the small hand clutching it and up the sleeve to the perpetrator. She should have known it was her younger brother.

"Charlie!" Mina whined and tried to swat the feather away. "Do you know how many diseases that feather is probably carrying, and you brought it into a hospital?"

Charlie just grinned wider and nodded his head. The eight-year-old proceeded to climb up onto Mina's hospital bed with an old pencil box. It usually housed his favorite possessions, like an old Matchbox car, a broken piece of quartz, silver bottle caps, a whistle, and a few old election pins. But currently these items weren't in the box but carefully placed around Mina's body on the hospital bed.

"Charlie, what are you doing?" She picked up the bottle cap that was closest to her hand and gave it back to her silent brother, who put it away in the box.

"He was worried about you," a warm voice answered from out in the hallway.

Mina's head spun toward the sound, and she almost cried in relief when she saw her mother standing there. Sara started crying, crossed to the hospital bed, and pulled her daughter and son into an embrace.

"Mom, I'm sorry. I never meant to make you worry." Mina sniffled.

"Shh, shh. It's okay," Sara intoned softly. "Well, no, it's not okay, but we will get to that later." She pulled away and brushed Mina's hair out of her face. "What happened? What were you thinking? When you didn't come home from school, I called Nan. She said you got a ride, but then when you didn't come home at all, I panicked. I was so scared, and I didn't know what to do. I thought maybe the Story had gotten involved and you were in the middle of a quest."

"Mom, it wasn't the Story, not exactly."

"I hate that you have to be a part of this. If there was any way that I could protect you from the Grimm curse you know I would, right?"

"You protected me for sixteen years from the curse and the Story. It's okay, Mom. Now it's my turn to protect Charlie and you." Mina tried to sound strong, but her words only made her mom tear up more.

"Oh, sweetheart. I can't tell you how helpless I felt, not knowing what was going on. The police wouldn't understand our circumstances…how could I call for help and tell them that I thought a fairy tale had come and kidnapped my daughter, or worse, killed her? I knew something had happened, but I couldn't do anything. I ended up calling the police, but they said you hadn't been missing for forty-eight hours." Sara stood up and paced the room, waving her hands wildly about.

"Mom!" Mina tried to distract her mother, knowing she was about to lose it.

"I mean, really! Forty-eight hours? Do they not have kids? Forty-eight hours to a scared parent might as well be forty-eight days." She stopped pacing, and Charlie jumped off the bed and began to put his knickknacks back in the box, obviously satisfied that they had served their purpose.

"Thanks, Charlie." Mina patted his head.

Charlie grinned and pointed his finger into his open palm.

Mina raised her eyebrow in disbelief. "I owe you? Why do I owe you?" She laughed.

Charlie started signing, and Mina watched carefully. "Because you protected me?"

Sara frowned at Charlie thoughtfully and spoke on his silent behalf. "Apparently, he read somewhere about creating a fairy circle for protection against evil. So he took all of his shiny objects and was adamant about protecting you. Even to the point of making a nuisance with the nurses."

"Oh," Mina whispered quietly.

Sara came and sat on the edge of her daughter's bed. "So tell me what happened."

"Mom, if I tell you, you are going to freak out and try to over-protect me, and you have to promise me that you will be calm, cool, and collected about what I say."

Sara pursed her lips and took a deep breath. "I don't know if I can guarantee that, but I will do my best."

Mina looked at her mother and started from the beginning. At first Sara was confused, then worried, and then angry. She had annoyed outbursts throughout Mina's story. *How dare he kidnap her daughter and chase her through the woods. How dare he spend the night in the woods with her daughter alone! And, finally, how dare he abandon her and leave her in the woods!* Mina found it quite funny the moods her mother went through: anger, indignation, and resentment.

"I don't care what happens, but you will stay away from that boy! Mina, he is nothing but trouble, and he's Fae to boot. You can't trust the Fae. I mean, just look at what he did to you! You could have been killed by bears out in those woods."

Mina began to laugh out loud, knowing how oblivious her mom was to what had happened. "Or in the city," she mumbled.

"No, I'm serious!" Sara tried to look serious, but her eyes slowly softened and she began to chuckle. "I'm just glad you're back and safe and sound. But why didn't the Grimoire work?"

Mina's eyes opened wide in panic. "Mom! Where's the Grimoire?" She looked down and realized she was in an ugly hospital gown.

Sara looked confused. "I don't know."

"Where are my clothes? Mom, we have to find my clothes!" Sara jumped up and went out the door to go look for a nurse with Charlie close on her heels. Mina was so worried she didn't hear the slight knock on the door.

"Oh! Well, what seems to have gotten our patient all worked up?" Mina looked up at the handsome doctor who'd spoken and was speechless; he looked familiar. It took a moment for Mina to put two and two together. It was Robert Martin, Nan's future stepdad.

Mina had to clear her throat a few times before she could speak. "My clothes — I want my clothes."

"Oh, I believe a nurse should have put those in a bag for you. I don't think they were salvageable." He spoke in a matter-of-fact tone.

"Oh, no, I needed something…" Mina paused, unsure of how to proceed without giving away too much information. Dr. Martin didn't seem to notice as he looked over her charts carefully.

He grinned at Mina, displaying very even and white teeth. His light brown hair had just a touch of grey at the temples, and his eyes were a deep hazel. "I'm sure that whatever it is, the nurses can get if for you. How are you feeling?"

"Mmm, good, I guess," Mina offered. "Thirsty and hungry, though."

"Not surprising with what you've been through. You came in with a fever, and you were dehydrated. But your fever broke last night, and other than your sprained ankle and a few deep cuts, you are on the mend."

"Wait, yesterday morning? How long have I been here? Wasn't I brought in last night?"

"Oh, your mom didn't tell you yet? You came in two nights ago. You've been unconscious with a fever for two days. It broke last night."

Mina sat stunned in her bed as Dr. Martin came and listened to her heart. Almost a week. She had missed almost a week of school.

Dr. Martin scribbled something on her file. "If you're ready, I'll have a nurse remove the I.V. You think you can handle soup?"

Mina nodded. Her stomach rumbled at the thought of food.

"Found it!" Sara came strolling into the room with a white plastic bag. She handed the bag to Mina, who tore it open and pulled out her jeans; she dug around in her pockets.

"Mom, it's not in my pockets!" Mina cried out.

"Well, maybe it fell out and is caught in the bag," she answered. They dumped the bag of dirty clothes on the bed and began to dig through everything. It wasn't there.

"Is everything all right?" Dr. Martin asked.

Mina felt uncomfortable at letting her emotions get the best of her in front of a complete stranger. "Um, no," she lied. "I seem to have lost something very important to me. Did you see a small leather book about yay big?" She held up her hands in the size of the Grimoire.

"Ah, no, I haven't, but I'll check with the emergency team," Dr. Martin answered briskly. "Hopefully, they may have it. But I see that your mom's already found the bag. Everything on you when you came in was in that bag. Maybe you lost it in the woods."

Mina's heart dropped, and Sara reached forward and grasped her daughter around the shoulders in a form of comfort. "It's okay, honey," Sara whispered reassuringly. "We'll find it."

This was turning out to be the absolute worst day ever. How was she going to overcome the quests if she didn't have the Grimoire to imprison the evil Fae in? She wasn't, that's how. She was doomed, just like her Uncle Jack.

"Oh, by the way, I've promised a few of your friends that they could visit, if you were well enough. We'll give you some time. Maybe after you eat."

"I don't know. I'm not sure I want to receive company?" Mina felt another moment of panic. Who could possibly be out in the hall?

"Even if it's my future stepdaughter?" Dr. Martin teased, and began laughing. "I can only waylay her so long before she bribes one of my nurses with cupcakes or sneaks in here anyway."

"Wait, Nan? Nan's here? Yes, I want to see Nan," Mina cried out excitedly.

"In a bit, after you eat," the doctor ordered. "She can wait that long. Although I'm sure she will be trying to sneak in, but I think she can hold on for another hour."

Mina grinned.

CHAPTER 12

It only took forty-five minutes before Nan maneuvered her way into Mina's hospital room. Sara and Charlie had left a half hour earlier in search of the lost and found, looking for the Grimoire. Mina had just finished her soup when Nan came sneaking in.

"You're late," Mina chirped. "I thought for sure you would sneak in here earlier."

Nan rolled her eyes. "I tried. I couldn't get past Nurse Dragon, and my future stepdad wasn't helping the matter. I think he purposely put old Dragon Lady on me so I wouldn't sneak in here."

"Well, then, how did you get in?"

"I got Charlie to knock over a cart at the end of the hall!" She grinned triumphantly and crossed her arms. "It made such a commotion that everyone went running." Nan lifted a backpack and put it on Mina's bed. "I brought you the emergency essentials: lip gloss, curling iron, hairspray, high heels — "

"Nan, I have crutches! I can't wear heels," Mina interrupted.

"Okay, scratch the heels. I'll wear the heels — you can wear my flats." She began to pull everything out of her bag and reached for Mina's hair.

Mina grabbed her best friend's wrists and pinned them down on the bed. "Nan, what's going on? Are we okay?" She felt terrible for the way she had acted and treated her best friend. "Can you ever forgive me for getting freaked out at the concert and wanting to go home? I shouldn't have abandoned you like that."

Nan's face became still, quiet. Then she erupted into a huge smile and hugged her closely. "No, I'm sorry for overreacting. I should've figured it was your way of getting some alone time with Brody. I can't believe I didn't think of it earlier. I know you have a crush on him." She grabbed Mina's hand and squeezed tightly. "Can you forgive me for hanging out with Savannah? I did it to kind of get back at you. I was still mad at the time. But as soon as I heard that you went missing, I grew up and realized how stupid I was. I'm your BFF through thick and thin."

Mina started crying and hugged her friend again. Nan leaned back and began to mess with the makeup and things she had brought in with her. "Nan?" Mina asked. "What's going on?"

Nan smiled at Mina. "You're on TV. I overheard one of the nurses talking. You probably didn't know this, but someone by the name of Jed Parsons was monitoring the old handheld radio channels and overheard a conversation about a young girl found lost in the woods."

"That was probably Karl calling in to tell people he found me," Mina inserted.

Nan raised her eyebrows skeptically. "Well, I don't know anything about that, except that old Jed thought it was serious and called for help, and since he knew his radio could only reach a few miles, he was able to tell the park rangers and rescue teams a general direction of where to look."

"It wouldn't have mattered. I was safe with Karl, and he had a radio and called for help." Mina tried to assure Nan that it wasn't a big deal.

"By the time you made it to the hospital, there was quite the stir, and there were news teams already waiting for you here." Nan began to bounce on the bed excitedly.

"I don't remember," Mina replied lamely.

"Of course, you didn't know. It was obvious from the footage that you were totally out of it. But it was so cool!" Nan gushed.

"It wasn't that big of a deal. Someone found me and then....I don't remember much after that." Mina touched her forehead in confusion.

"What time is it?" Nan looked at the clock on the wall. "Here, watch this — they've been replaying it over the last two days." Nan grabbed the remote control from the hospital nightstand and furiously clicked away at the black box until the TV came to life. After a few hurried groans from Nan and more channel surfing, she squealed, "There you are!"

Mina watched numbly as a female news reporter dressed in a light jacket with a blue umbrella spoke in a mellow voice that showed little emotion. "Here behind me we see the rescue of one Wilhelmina Grime, who was lost in the Mt. Adams National Forest. The girl, a sophomore at Kennedy High, was last seen after school with friends. How she ended up lost in the forest is still unknown. A mysterious call by Jed Parsons into the Parks Services led to a quick rescue."

The cameraman panned to the ambulance as Mina was loaded on a stretcher with the help of the emergency techs. It was obvious from the way her head flopped from side to side that she was passed out from exhaustion.

The camera and a different reporter pushed through and tried to shove a microphone in her face. "Mina, can you tell us how you became lost in the woods? Were you kidnapped? Held as hostage?"

The camera zoomed in close to Mina's mud-streaked face. Someone tried to push the microphone away from Mina, but not before it picked up her delirious whisper of one word. Mina in her unconscious state called out one name. One very audible boy's name, and it wasn't one she was expecting. She called out Jared's name.

Mina froze in her hospital room and prayed that the reporter hadn't understood her. But the reporter was fast. She was able to pick up Mina's whispered name, and she repeated it into the mic. "Who is this Jared? And if you know him, you'd better tell him that Wilhelmina Grime is calling for him."

"EEEEK!" Mina screamed into her hospital blanket as she watched herself on the small TV. She couldn't have believed it, wouldn't have believed it, if she hadn't just seen it with her own two eyes. The news report was proof that she was completely insane. Well, hopefully no one would know that she was speaking about the Jared from her school. What if people got the wrong idea? What if Brody heard?

Mina crumpled onto the bed and pulled the thin blanket over her head to hide herself from the world. She could hear the obnoxious reporter speak again, only this time it was a current broadcast, and it sounded like she was broadcasting from outside the hospital. Groaning, Mina pulled down the blanket enough to see the screen and a group of kids from her school leaving flowers, posters, and cards by the hospital for her. She was touched — she didn't think anyone even knew who she was, but here was proof of their fondness for her. What happened next completely changed her mind.

The reporter, whose name was Brandy Westhouse, appeared next to the serious and demure face of none other than Savannah White. "So how do you know Wilhelmina?"

Savannah's face looked forlorn with faked sadness. "We are friends at Kennedy High. Best friends, and I'm devastated at what happened. Wilhelmina is sweet and didn't deserve to have something bad like this happen to her." Savannah sniffed and wiped fake tears away with a Kleenex. Mina rolled her eyes and would've given a million dollars to see if the hanky was actually wet. Savannah continued. "I only wish that I could've taken her place."

"HA!" Nan yelled at the screen. "You're only saying that because you wish it were you lost in the woods so you can get all of the attention. You crazy attention addict! Can you believe the nerve of her, saying she's your best friend and she doesn't even know that you prefer Mina, not Wilhelmina. Geesh!"

"When did that interview happen?" Mina pointed at the screen.

"Oh, just this afternoon. The hospital has been really good at keeping the crazies away and giving you a bit of peace."

"They didn't keep you away," Mina remarked dryly.

"That's because they don't have a meter able to measure my amount of craziness. Plus, I just told hospital security that I was supposed to bring my future stepdad his lunch. They all know me by name now, so the security and front desk didn't blink an eye. But the head floor nurse, Dierdre, aka Dragon Lady, she was another story." Nan shuddered.

The news story changed on the TV, and a picture of a middle-aged gentleman wearing a brown UPS uniform flashed on the screen. Mina read the words carefully that scrolled across the bottom. Dan Williams, a local UPS worker, had disappeared during his morning route. His truck was left running on Main Street, but no one had seen him. A tip line number appeared if anyone had any information about his disappearance.

"Oh, my goodness, that's horrible! I can't watch this anymore." Nan clicked off the television with the remote. "By the way, are you hungry?" She reached over to pull out a brown paper sack and the sandwich that was inside.

"But I thought that was for Dr. Martin?"

"No way, are you kidding me? Do you know how much he makes? He can afford to buy his own lunch." Nan took a large bite out of one half of the turkey sandwich and handed the other to Mina, who quickly took a small bite.

Loud footsteps interrupted their picnic, and Nan scrambled to hide the evidence of their lunch. She shoved the food back into the bag and thrust it under Mina's pillow. Mina had just enough time to wipe her face with the sleeve of her gown when her mother and a chagrined-looking Charlie entered.

"You! Sit over there and don't move." Sara pointed to a chair, and Charlie walked slowly, dragging his feet dramatically, as if walking to his own execution. Sara's brown hair was pulled into a ponytail, and she looked frazzled. Charlie sat down on the chair and gave Nan a knowing grin. When Sara looked up, she was surprised to see Nan.

"Oh, hello, Nan."

"Hello, Mrs. Grime," Nan chirped merrily.

Nurse Diedre walked in, gave Nan an angry glare, and went to the bed and unhooked Mina's I.V. Nan scooted quickly out of the grey-haired nurse's way and went to lounge on the chair next to Charlie. Nan sat texting on her phone while Charlie played with the items in his box; the whole while Mina tried to make small talk with the nurse.

The nurse refused to smile, talk, or comment, and her bedside manner was terrible. Nan was right. The nurse really was mean.

But the cream of chicken soup, with the help of the forbidden sandwich, really gave Mina her strength back. She felt so good that she let her best friend brush her hair and paint her fingernails an obnoxious purple that only Nan could pull off.

Sara's phone beeped, and she went into the hall to answer it. A few minutes later she stepped back in, her face scrunched up with anger.

"I'm sorry, honey. That was my boss. There seems to be a problem with one of the houses I clean, and she demanded that I come right away. I told her that my daughter is in the hospital, but she was quite insistent. Do you think you will be all right with Nan, alone? I can pick up some more clothes for you, too. Is there anything in particular you want?"

Mina made a shooing motion. "I'm not going anywhere until the doctor says I can. I'll be fine — just grab any old pair of jeans and a shirt that's clean." Sara hugged Mina before she and Charlie left.

A few minutes later, Nan, bored out of her mind, went looking for some magazines and left Mina alone. Grateful for the solitude and the silence that came with it, she leaned back in her bed and stared out the window across the hospital campus. She couldn't help but admire the architecture of the brand-new hospital.

The Memorial Hospital had only been open for six months and was the result of copious very rich backers. Where most hospitals were square and made of boring brick, this one was configured like the number eight and made of beautiful reflective glass. It had a soothing flow to the layout because there were no hard edges or corners to any of the rooms. There were two botanical gardens in the center of each "eight," giving every room a relaxing, luxurious view. It was a hospital designed for the rich and famous and purposely designed to not resemble a hospital.

When Nan didn't come back right away, Mina had time to reflect on the recent events, Mina couldn't help but feel her cheeks burn with embarrassment at the thought of calling out Jared's name while she was unconscious. She'd probably said it because he was the last thing on her mind. Hopefully, Brody wouldn't see that. Her heart began to break again at the thought of what they'd shared and lost. It was like a horrible Greek tragedy.

A tear slowly escaped Mina's eyes, and she quickly wiped it away. She ached for him, ached for him to hold her hand, to kiss her. She even missed the sound of his voice. Even now, in a hospital surrounded by machines, she could still imagine the soft baritone of Brody Carmichael's voice whispering her name.

Closing her eyes in pain, she bit her lip and whispered, "Stop it. Go away."

Mina spoke out loud to her overactive imagination. She literally thought she was going crazy. She was hearing his voice and it sounded so real. It was like he was right next to her.

"But I thought you would like company," the voice answered her back.

Mina's eyes flew open, and she gasped in surprise. Brody Carmichael stood next to her bed with a bouquet of flowers.

CHAPTER 13

The flowers were birds of paradise. He walked over and placed them next to the get-well carnations that her mother had brought. Brody's birds of paradise made her mother's flowers look cheap and drab, another reminder of the difference in their stations in life.

He turned to her, his hands hanging limply at his sides. He tried to clear his throat a few times before he spoke. It was apparent he was more nervous than she was.

Subconsciously, Mina's hand flew to her heart as if she could slow its wild beating. She was sure that he could hear it beating, it was so fast.

Gathering his nerves, he spoke first. "How are you?" He didn't move closer; it was as if he were scared. His blond hair looked as if he had run his hands through it multiple times, and his eyes were filled with worry.

"I'm good," Mina whispered, too scared to say anything more to the perfect boy in front of her.

The tension that was evident in Brody's entire body evaporated at her words. "Good, I'm glad." He looked down at his hands and put them in his jean pockets. Mina wondered vaguely if they were six-hundred-dollar jeans.

He continued to look down at his feet, afraid to look her in the eye, when he asked the next question. "Why?...Why did you call out his name?"

"Who-what?" Mina stumbled over her words, shocked at what she was hearing.

Brody's eyes shot up from the ground to look her in the eyes, daring her to look away.

"I'm sorry. This is not how I planned to ask you. Are you two dating? Seeing each other?" He looked hurt, confused.

Mina felt like a stone plummeted to the bottom of her stomach, taking all of her bravery with it. "I don't know what you're talking about," she fumbled back.

"You said *his* name. I heard it, clear as day, on the news. I even recorded it and watched it over and over again. What I want to know is why?"

Mina's hands started to shake. She closed her eyes and turned away, unwilling to look at him. Unable to tell him what she knew, and unable to lie about her feelings, it became too much, and one silent tear slid unbidden down her cheek.

Brody stepped back in shock from her tear before moving forward and closing the distance between them. He began to reach for her hand but pulled back, unsure of what to do. "I'm sorry! I didn't mean to upset you. I'm just confused by what's happened lately. And it seems to be a lot, and I can't seem to control my emotions."

Mina tried to form a coherent thought and sentence, but it hurt so much to be so near him and not be able to tell him how she felt.

"No one believes me, but I'm cursed." She hadn't meant to say it, but it came rushing out without a thought.

He looked relieved when she was able to speak. "Hey, you're not cursed. You're alive, right? I would say that makes you extremely lucky, not cursed." He became eerily quiet.

Brody pulled over a hospital chair so that it was next to her bed, and he relaxed into the seat. He grabbed a magazine that Nan had left and began to thumb through it without really looking at it.

"Why are you here?" Mina asked him, confused by his casual demeanor and willingness to sit in someone's hospital room.

Brody's finger caught in a page, and he closed the magazine and locked eyes with her. "I don't know. I was hoping you could tell me."

Mina shook her head in confusion. "You're the one who drove to the hospital, got in past security and the nurses — I'm still not sure how you did that — and walked into my room, not the other way around. You should know your reason for being here, not me."

Brody smirked in the familiar way that made Mina's heart melt. "But here I am." He held up his arms in a casual way. "You're someone I barely know, and yet, when I heard you had gone missing, I felt as if my whole world turned upside down. It's been haunting me for two nights straight. I can barely eat, sleep, think, and finally I came to the conclusion that you would know why. Do you have a spell on me?"

"I think you must have read one too many fairy tales," Mina answered quickly, blushing. Immediately, she regretted her choice of words.

Brody shook his head. "This girl from my school, who obviously is strong enough to survive on her own out in the wilderness, miraculously gets saved. And the one name she calls out to in her time of need happens to be the only guy in school that, for some crazy reason, I absolutely hate!" Brody's body tensed up, and he slowly frowned at her. "I don't consider myself a jealous person, but I barely know Jared, and I really, really don't like him. And the thought of you and him together makes me want to punch something. Especially when I have no right to feel that way about Jared, or you. It's as if we met somewhere..." He trailed off.

"No, it's not what you think," Mina said, rushing to her own defense.

"How do you know what I'm thinking?" Brody stood up, walked over to Mina, and leaned down, placing both hands on either side of her body, pinning her between his muscled arms. He was so close Mina could smell his familiar aftershave.

She looked up at his jaw line and swallowed before turning her head away from him and playing with the seam on the blanket, trying anything to appear more interested in the hospital blanket than his closeness, his jaw, his lips.

"Tell me, why do I have this sudden urge to hold you, to kiss you, when I barely know you?" Brody pulled away in disgust. "What's wrong with me? You must think I'm some kind of crazed psychopath, talking like this. I come into your room unasked and start to demand answers to some crazy questions that I'd hoped you would have answers to. I can't help but think something is wrong with me, that I really am going crazy." He turned his back on her and ran his hands through his hair again in frustration.

Mina licked her lips nervously. "Maybe you're cursed, too?"

Brody sighed heavily and looked over his shoulder at her. "I must be — why else would I be here?"

Those words drove straight to Mina's heart like a wooden stake. They hurt, but there was truth in those words. Brody could be being manipulated by the Story once again. It made Mina angry. Angry at the world, at the Fae, at how unfair everything was for a sixteen-year-old girl in love. He began to move toward to door.

"Brody, wait!" she called out.

Brody froze, his hand on the door, his back stiff, waiting for the ball to drop.

"I wish it was your name," she blurted out. "I wish it was your name that I had called out." She waited in anticipation, hoping he would turn around, run to her and kiss her like he said he wanted to. He didn't turn around.

His broad shoulders relaxed, and his head bent forward to look at the ground. "I wish you did, too," he choked out. "Can you tell me why I feel this way? Can you tell me what's wrong with me?"

Mina's heart soared with the prospect of telling Brody EVERYTHING! She opened her mouth to explain when a mirror image startled her. In the reflection of the window, she saw Jared, and he looked scared. She looked over her shoulder, but he wasn't there in the room with her. She glanced back toward the window, and his reflection was faint, far off. It looked like Jared was speaking to her; his mouth was moving, but she couldn't hear anything. He was trying to warn her about something.

She turned to Brody to see if he had noticed, but he still had his back to the window. Mina looked toward the window again, but Jared was gone. And with him went the message he was trying to get to her. But it gave her just enough pause. What she did was dangerous, and because she cared for Brody, she *shouldn't* involve him. But it was because she thought she might love Brody that she *wouldn't* involve him.

Reluctantly, she dropped her chin to her chest and sighed out loud. He was still patiently waiting for an answer. When one didn't immediately come forth, his posture stiffened again.

"I see," he said.

No other words were spoken by either one of them because Brody left the room.

CHAPTER 14

Having to stay off her sprained ankle made it impossible for Mina to make it up the fire escape to her garden refuge on top of her apartment building. She waited on her window bench, staring dolefully out into the night. There wasn't much to look at, since her room faced the adjoining building and the window of Mrs. Orn, the neighborhood cat lady. Her visitors included Mr. and Mrs. Wong from the restaurant downstairs, who brought her dumplings; Nan; and the errant news reporter.

After the fourth knock on their door by reporters wanting to do interviews, Sara Grime was becoming unraveled. Mina's mom didn't know how she was supposed to protect her daughter from the curse when everyone in the world was somehow able to find them, despite being unlisted. The very observant Mrs. Wong dragged large bamboo mats and tall plants out of her restaurant to the curb. She covered the entrance to the stairwell with the tall mat and placed various plants and vases in front, making it look like a beautiful display.

She then sat outside with a tray of free samples of orange chicken, and in broken English distracted the rest of the reporters by purposely giving them wrong directions to her house. Her behavior was a complete one-eighty compared to a few months ago, when she had made a collage of newspaper articles about Mina and plastered them to her storefront window, bragging how a famous celebrity lived above her. Maybe because this wasn't exciting news but more of a tragedy that brought out the protective instincts of the small Chinese woman, but whatever her reasons, the Grime family were grateful for their paparazzi protector.

But it wasn't long before the news reporters forgot about the girl lost in the woods and turned to reporting on bigger stories. A local DMV worker had disappeared during the night. At first, a few people wrote it off as an unfortunate government employee being unhappy with their benefits. The next day, a young female coffee barista from the local Starbucks disappeared as well.

Three people in as many days disappeared without a trace. People began to talk and spread gossip, and rumors arose of possible kidnappings, but since no ransom notes were found, and no bodies were discovered, the media and police downplayed the "trend" as individual runaway cases.

Mina barely kept up with the news because she still hadn't found the Grimoire and was at her wits' end. If it wasn't for her mother, who made sure Mina left her house to go to the doctor's and school, Mina would have become a hermit, too scared to go anywhere.

Dr. Martin gave Mina explicit instructions, and she had to wear a brace and use the crutches as much as possible for a week. Much to her dismay, her school was almost impossible to navigate. Her crutches kept getting knocked accidentally by stray bags and shoes, and Mina would find herself on her back, looking at the putrid yellow paint of the hall ceilings.

Thankfully, Nan was there to yell insults at the boys who obliviously knocked into her. She also turned every embarrassing tumble into a comical adventure by creating a photo tally. Mina's fall count had risen to four, and it wasn't even lunch.

"Ooh, that fall was the best — I think you got air on that one." Nan pulled Mina up and dusted off her bottom and back. "You ready?" she asked. Nan carefully pulled the phone in front of her, and Mina made a face and held up five fingers, symbolizing the fifth fall. "Cheese!"

Mina tried to smile, but all she was able to bear was a painful grin. Nan grabbed up Mina's books, put them in her locker, and helped her get in line for lunch.

The lunchroom was crowded, and the roar of people eating and talking mellowed to a quiet din as she entered. People stared, pointed, and whispered in their direction. When Mina pretended ignorance and didn't do anything interesting or spectacular, they returned to eating their mediocre lunches. She was used to this pattern of silence then ignorance; it had already happened in each of her earlier classes.

Some meaningful students who wanted fame tried to offer help to Mina, but Nan scared them all away. After all, she didn't want fair-weather friends or, as Nan called them, storm-chaser friends — people who only wanted to be her friend because of the publicity they would get by being associated with her.

Mina tried to pick out her own food, but Nan was too busy talking about the finale of her favorite show to pay attention. Nan selected two deli sandwiches, cookies, milk, an apple, and bags of chips. Mina sighed when Nan switched topics to rave about Valdemar. After making their way through the hectic maze of chairs and tables, she was able to seek shelter at her favorite lunch table.

Even knowing that Brody was in the same room that she was didn't make her feel any better. He came in, filled his tray with food, passed all of his friends, and sat at a table by himself facing Mina. His posture and furrowed brows betrayed that he was in no mood to be friendly.

Nan noticed his brooding and made a comment about it to Mina. "What's wrong with Captain Popular today?"

Brody picked up his fork and stared at Mina, ignoring all conversation directed his way from his friends. T.J. tried to talk to him, but Brody brushed him off. Savannah even tried to catch his eye, but nothing she did could hold a flame to the angry glare he kept directing toward Nan and Mina.

Mina more than anyone understood what Brody was probably thinking. But she never expected to be the recipient of his indifference, and it totally discomforted her. She squirmed, fidgeted, and found it impossible to even open up her milk carton while he looked at her. Her nerves made it impossible for her to eat, and if he didn't stop it, she was going to go hungry.

Nan noticed. "Brody Carmichael!" she hissed out loud. "Where are your manners? You should know better than to upset someone who is in a very delicate state right now." Nan had taken on a thick southern accent while she reprimanded Brody.

Brody was completely taken aback by Nan's abruptness.

Mina grabbed the edge of Nan's striped shirt and pulled hard, trying to get her attention.

Nan picked up Mina's food and put it on her own lunch tray, and headed out the lunchroom doors. Mina followed behind slowly, being careful to not look around or behind her at the open-mouthed Brody.

"Nan, wait up," Mina hissed when she entered the hallway and couldn't find her friend.

"Over here!" Nan called out as she poked her head out of the unlocked biology classroom.

Mina entered the class and sat on the stool at one of the lab stations while Nan redistributed their lunch. She was angry, and kept squishing and damaging their food as she tried to separate their lunches. Mina ended up with two broken cookies, a crushed bag of chips, and a very shaken-up carton of two-percent milk.

"The nerve of him!" Nan fumed. "Doesn't he realize how lucky we are to have you here? There was no reason whatsoever for him to glare at us like that." She tried to pull the wrapper off her straw and stab it into her own carton of milk before she realized she had Mina's chocolate milk.

Deftly Mina switched their milk cartons back as Nan continued her rant. "I mean, for goodness' sake, Mina! Your face could have ended up on a milk carton if you weren't found!" Nan held the carton an inch from her face.

"Nan," Mina soothed, "it's fine. Brody's only angry because we had an argument. I think he is just confused. He actually came to the hospital and visited me."

When Nan's eyes went wide in disbelief and her mouth dropped open to comment on Brody personally coming to see her friend, Mina quickly changed the subject. "And besides, they don't put kids' faces on milk cartons anymore."

Nan's blonde eyebrows furrowed in speculation, and she began to scrutinize her own milk carton. "Are you sure? I thought I saw it in a movie somewhere."

Mina laughed out loud, "I'm sure, if anything, it would have been an Amber alert."

"Oh," Nan said somewhat dejectedly. "I would have liked to see your face on a milk carton."

"Nan Taylor!" Mina guffawed and shook her head. "What is wrong with you?"

Nan's face lit up with a mischievous grin. "That's what you get for not telling me about Brody! You don't think you can avoid the question that easily. How come you didn't tell me that the prince of hotness visited you in the hospital? Where was I, by the way?"

Mina fumbled a bit. "I think you were out looking for a magazine."

"But I'm your best friend. Don't you think you should have told me? It's not like I would have teased you about it — much." She did a beautiful pout, and Mina couldn't help but apologize to Nan.

"I'm sorry — I was surprised and caught off guard."

"It's because you like him, I know." Nan sighed and leaned her head on her hand. "He has almost as many hot points as Valdemar. Well, I think they are tied for hot points. On a scale of one to ten, they are a definite twelve."

Mina took a bite of her cookie. "But the scale only goes to ten," she mumbled through the crumbs.

"Not with hot points," Nan explained. "You get an extra bonus point for being rich, and one for being a celebrity. And since that covers both of them, that would make them a twelve."

"Well, that doesn't do us much good, since we're not twelves."

Nan began to pick all of the M&Ms off her cookie and popped them into her mouth one by one. "Nonsense. We rank high in cute points."

Mina raised her eyebrow in disbelief. "'Cute points'?"

"Duh, the cute points are better than hot points. We rate high in cute points. We are funny, quirky, have great personalities, and are extremely charming." She batted her eyelashes comically. "These are way more important than hot points."

"How so?" Mina asked, dumbfounded.

"Well, girls who rank high in hot points will eventually get old and will no longer be hot, so their hot points get lower. If you have cute points, they last forever, even when you are old. So they are definitely way more important."

Mina almost choked on her cookie, she was laughing so hard. Nan always had a different way of looking at the world. They finished their lunch by discussing the hot versus cute point ratings for all of the kids in their class.

It wasn't until Mina caught movement over her best friend's shoulder that her smile died on her lips. Every muscle in her body tensed as a familiar tingling raced up her spine, her only warning that something magical was at work.

The movement came again, and she tried to pretend indifference to the fluttering movements coming from the locked biology cabinet. She knew what was stored in that particular glass cabinet. She had seen the preserved bodies of the chickens and frogs, and even a two-headed pig. Year after year, they had been floating lifeless in their jars of formaldehyde.

The Kennedy students had even nicknamed the two-headed pig Twinky. Mina never gave credit to the names and preferred to ignore the creatures suspended in their liquid glass coffins. But she could no longer ignore them, because the dead specimens were moving. Twinky himself, with both heads, started to struggle in the jar. His mouth opened wide, and she could almost hear the silent squeals echoing in the classroom.

She faltered mid-sentence with Nan, and quickly began to gather up her uneaten lunch. Mina glanced out of the corner of her eye to see one of the frogs swimming happily back in forth in his jar.

Nan complained, "Hey, I'm not done with that." She tried to snatch another chip from Mina's tray.

"No, we are definitely done," Mina shot out hurriedly. She tried to pick up the tray and turn Nan toward the door and away from lab cabinet, which was now shaking slightly from the frenzied movement coming from within.

But Mina wasn't able to carry the trays and both crutches, and she began to lose the tray and all of the food on it. Nan caught the trays and dumped them into the nearest trash can. "If you really wanted to get out of here, you could have just told me," she answered, somewhat annoyed.

Mina was proud of her recovery. "I just remembered. I overheard a senior saying that they were dissecting various brains on these tables today." It was an obvious lie, but one that seemed to get Nan moving in the direction of the door.

"Oh, that is disgusting! I should have never even brought our lunch in here. I'm surprised we could eat with all of those Frankenstein animals in the cabinet anyway."

Nan had just begun to turn her head and point at the aforementioned cabinet when Mina heard a distinct clicking sound. Without looking, she knew it was the chicken tapping his beak on the jar, desperately trying to break free. She pushed Nan bodily through the door as the clicking sound grew louder.

"Did you hear something?" Nan turned and tried to crane her neck back into the classroom.

"Nope," Mina answered quickly, too quickly.

"I thought I heard tapping?" Nan looked at Mina.

"Uh, you did." Mina began to tap her fingers impatiently against the metal support of her crutch.

Nan's head tilted to the side. "No, I could have sworn it sounded like glass." Nan couldn't press the argument further because the first warning bell rang.

Mina closed the lab door firmly behind her and started a frenzied hopping toward her next class, hoping Nan would follow her lead. She didn't. Mina stopped when she realized Nan wasn't behind her. She turned and looked over her shoulder at her blonde best friend, who hadn't moved from her spot outside the biology lab door.

Nan's face was furrowed in confusion as if she was listening intently for something, but it was obvious she couldn't hear anything over the sound of rushing feet and slamming lockers. She made a move toward the door as if to open it.

Mina was helpless and stared at her friend in horror. What could she do? Thinking fast, she pretended to fall again, but this time with fanfare. She was so desperate to gain attention she even threw her crutch into the path of an oncoming student and screamed loudly as she flopped hard on her butt on the cold, hard floor, right in the middle of the hallway.

Her cheeks burned with embarrassment as Frank, the unlucky student tripped by her wayward crutch, fell on top of her.

"Ouch!" Mina cried out.

"Sorry! Oof, sorry again," Frank mumbled as he tried to extract himself from the mess of his tangled backpack, Mina's crutch, and the hands that came out of nowhere to help them up. But the spectacle did its job, as Nan released the biology door handle and raced to rescue her.

After the incident and the gawkers cleared the hallway, Nan smiled brightly and pulled out her camera phone.

"Six!" she laughed while pointing it at both of them, and clicked the phone.

.

CHAPTER 15

A knock sounded at the door. Mina and Charlie were spread out on the floor playing a card game, and both looked at each other expectantly.

"You get it," Mina stated.

Charlie smirked at his sister, crossed his arms, and shook his head no.

"Charlie, I'm on crutches. It's not like I'm going cheat and look at your cards when you turn your back," Mina lied.

His hands flew in the air so fast Mina had problems understanding him. "Yeah, but that was only the one time." He continued signing. "Okay, *and* I cheated at Uno." When he didn't stop, Mina had to interrupt. "All right, I cheat at *all* card games. But if *you* don't catch me, is it really cheating?" She laughed.

The knocking at the door continued; Charlie glared at Mina, picked up every single one of his cards, and carried them with him to the door. He made a wide berth around Mina, keeping the cards to his chest as he passed by. Mina swung playfully at his cards, trying to knock them out of his hands.

Whoever was at the door was becoming impatient, and Mina heard a key being inserted into the lock. Mina's hand clutched the crutch on the floor next to her to use as a weapon. The door swung open, and a very small Chinese woman entered with her hands full. It was Mrs. Wong, their landlord.

"Meehna, you keep me waiting. You won't get your get betteh dumplins if you don't geht over here." Mrs. Wong shuffled into their small kitchen carrying a large pot and a small cloth grocery bag. Charlie forgot about the card game and jumped into the kitchen chair, awaiting with anticipation the food Mrs. Wong began to pull out and place on the table.

Mrs. Wong and her husband owned the entire building and the Chinese restaurant underneath the Grimes' home. At first Mina hated it, because if someone forgot to close their windows at night, their clothes would usually smell like Chinese food. But now Mina couldn't imagine living anywhere else, for the Wongs were almost like surrogate grandparents for Mina and her brother, and spoiled them with presents every holiday and all-they-can-eat dumplings the rest of the year, which for a cash-strapped family was a very welcome blessing.

"Ahh, Meehna, why you not reesting? You should be lying down, getting stronger so you can go get a cute boy, eh?" Mrs. Wong never missed a beat in her chatter about Mina's nonexistent love life as she made her way comfortably around their kitchen, pulling out dishes and silverware while setting the table. Mina hobbled over to the kitchen table to join her brother and continued to receive plenty of unwanted dating advice. She opened up the container of dumplings and put a whole one in her mouth and listened halfheartedly to Mrs. Wong's rants.

She berated Mina for not finding a guy as handsome as her husband, Mr. Wong. "You get nice guy like my Riu, see, and you won't ever be left alone in woods again. Dat Jared boy, he be bad news."

Mina started to choke on her dumpling in shock. Mrs. Wong never lost a beat as she began to hit her very hard on the back until the piece of food became dislodged from Mina's windpipe. Mina and her mom had never told anyone about Jared abandoning her because he was Fae and they didn't want any more trouble on their hands than they already had. So it was never mentioned in the papers or on the news — nothing. Maybe it was because Mrs. Wong lived in the same building and no one could have secrets with her around. Or maybe she had seen Mina and Jared on the roof last week. Mina wanted to ask more questions, but the door opened again as Sara came in with some groceries.

Sara was extremely excited about the meal. "Oh, Mei, what a wonderful surprise! Thank you so much." Sara walked over and gave the diminutive Chinese woman a hug.

Mrs. Wong spoke quickly in Chinese and then translated. "I heard about Meehna. She needs good food to help geet well, quick now."

When Sara was preoccupied with putting her own groceries away, Mrs. Wong hobbled over quietly to Mina. She reached into her apron and pulled out a small white envelope with a Chinese character written in gold ink inscribed across the front. "Here, drink this tonight. It will make you strong like me." She patted her chest encouragingly. "It secret family recipe, heal bettah than doctor medicine. Good good." She brought one finger slowly up to her lips and winked at Mina.

Confused, Mina opened her mouth to speak, but Mrs. Wong whisked across the room, taking her bags with her. In a flutter of broken English and Chinese, she pointedly ignored all of Mina's efforts to gain her attention again.

Sara tried to help set the table with food, but Mrs. Wong wouldn't have it. She kept swatting Sara's hands away and made numerous annoyed comments in Chinese under her breath. When she was happy that the table was set to her extremely high standards and everything was in order, she said her quick goodbyes and left the apartment, giving Mina a wide berth.

Stunned, Mina fingered the small packet under the table and kept running her fingers over the gold character. She wanted to ask Mei Wong about it, or even her mother, but that wasn't what the Chinese woman probably had in mind when she purposely gave it to her without her mother's knowledge. For all she knew it could be poison, but then again, the Wongs had never shown anything but goodwill toward the Grime family.

When Mina was sure that Mrs. Wong wasn't going to change her mind and walk in on them again, she decided it was time to tell her mother about her incident at school.

"Mom, it's starting again." Mina tried to sound very nonchalant as she stirred her hot bowl of soup.

"What is, dear?" Sara asked. She opened up a container of lo mein noodles and scooped out a portion to an eagerly awaiting Charlie.

Mina stabbed up a piece of orange chicken with her fork and blew on it. "Oh, you know, stuff, with a capital 'S.'" She took a bite of her rice.

Sara's hand froze in mid-air. Her inner turmoil was evident on her face and her shaking hands, but both of the Grime women were experts at hiding their emotions from Charlie. Sara swallowed nervously but continued to portion out the rest of the food.

"Ah, I see."

"Yeah, my, um, biology class was interesting. And let's just say that not everyone agreed with the stuff in the specimen jars. Let's just say they were very...animated." Mina let the words hang in the air.

She watched Charlie sit in his chair, wearing his normal plethora of superhero costume pieces, which included a Hulk shirt and a Batman utility belt and cape. His small feet, wearing his favorite rain boots, kicked back and forth happily. He made overly loud slurping noises while sucking up the noodles, and when he was finished, he grinned at Mina.

In no way was Charlie dumb, but there were certain things Sara never wanted to discuss with Charlie in the room for fear of worrying him. Mina had convinced her mother that they couldn't run anymore, that she needed to take her place as a Grimm and do her part to break the curse on her family by completing the quests. Reluctantly, Sara agreed, but she had conditions. One of those conditions was never to alarm Charlie if possible.

Sara patted Charlie's head affectionately. "Anything I should be overly concerned with?" Her brown eyes began to fill with tears, but she hid them well by getting up to get a gallon of milk out of the fridge. Mina could see her mother furiously wipe at them with her apron before approaching the table. When she sat down, Sara was solemn, with only a hint of red-rimmed eyes.

"Nope. It was just a small problem. Nothing bigger has presented itself." Mina tried to hide her words. One time she had entered a pet store and all of the animals began to behave erratically: trying to get out of cages, birds speaking terrible warnings to her. Other times, she would be followed by geese as if she was the original storybook goose girl.

"I was hoping for more time between…and then since we never found the Grimoire…" Sara trailed off. She sat at the table silently for the next few minutes, watching her children eat, before picking up her uneaten bowl of egg drop soup and putting it in the sink.

Mina knew better than to say anything else, so she waited and watched as her mother furiously cleaned up her own dishes, put the leftovers away, and then retired to her room, complaining of a headache.

Charlie immediately jumped up from the table and ran over to the small living room, flipped on the TV, and engrossed himself with Justice League of America cartoons.

Left sitting alone, Mina looked into her bowl of soup and found herself unable to eat anything else. Leaving her bowl on the table, she awkwardly got up and hopped to her small bedroom.

Even though Sara cleaned houses for a living, she never dared to enter Mina's domain and clean her teenage daughter's disaster zone. There were piles of clean laundry, dirty laundry, and magazines all over the floor. Mina tried to navigate the maze of mess that was her bedroom with a crutch, and she secretly wished she had cleaned her room.

She wheeled out her chair and sat at her garage-sale desk, which was badly in need of a new coat of stain, but she never got around to painting it. She opened the vellum envelope and was surprised to see it contained nothing more than a single tea bag. Mina pulled out the tea bag and studied it carefully, trying to identify the components of the leaves, but nothing struck her as out of the ordinary. Since everything looked the same, she flipped the switch on her hot pot and waited for the water to boil.

The hot pot was one of the greatest inventions since the toaster and Pop Tarts, and Mina used hers almost daily. She found a cup that looked clean, wiped it out, carefully poured the hot water into the ceramic mug, and slowly added the tea bag, stirring it around. Mina expected the water to turn a slight green or brown color from the color of the leaves; it didn't. Gold seeped out of the tea bag, floating and shimmering across the top of the water, reflecting the evening light.

Mina was scared to breathe, and watched as the flecks spun and twirled around the cup before slowly sinking to disappear under the water. The ceramic cup suddenly became too hot to hold. She almost dropped it, but recovered quickly and put the cup down on her desk, rubbing her slightly burned palms on her jeans. The tea bag continued to steep, but the steam from the cup dissipated rapidly, to be replaced by frost that slowly spread up the outside of the cup.

Mina pushed herself away from the desk and the cursed tea in shock. Her wheeled chair only made it a few feet before tangling in a pile of dirty clothes and tipping over, throwing her to the floor. She looked up, breathing heavily, and continued to half scoot, half crawl away from the aberrant phenomenon. When she reached her bed, she pulled her knees up to her chest and watched the cup warily. She was positive that at any moment it would shatter into a million pieces. When minutes passed and the cup continued to sit there unchanged, she decided to inspect it further.

She untangled the wheels of the chair from her jeans, damaging a favorite pair in the process, and sat back at the desk. Slowly she scooted forward, inch by inch, to inspect the cup. The frost was gone! Maybe she had imagined it. She grabbed a plastic spoon and stuck it into the cup, half expecting it to be melted into nothingness when she pulled it out. The spoon was fine. Confused, she sniffed the cup, and it smelled like normal Earl Grey tea.

A slight breeze made the papers on her desk shuffle, and Mina glanced at her bedroom window next to the desk and realized it was open. She reached over and shut the window. Maybe it was the sudden chill of the wind on the hot tea that made condensation appear on the outside of the cup. Maybe it wasn't frost at all; it very well could just be her overactive imagination.

Gathering her courage, she dipped one finger into the tea and brought it to her mouth to taste. The tea was slightly sweet, with a hint of spice that lingered, odd because she hadn't even added sugar or honey. After a moment of hesitation, she threw caution to the wind and decided to drink the tea. After all, Mrs. Wong would never ever give her something that would harm her. Maybe it was a quaint Asian home remedy or something.

The tea made Mina's body relax; her eyelids became heavy. Yawning, she crawled onto her bed, being sure to put an extra pillow under her swollen ankle to keep it raised. She was hoping that she could take the air cast off soon, but the doctor had told her it would be at least a week. It was only seven o'clock, but Mina couldn't keep her eyes open anymore. She lost the fight and fell asleep.

~~~

"Mina, where are the crutches?" Nan asked as she put her purse and Chapstick back into her locker. It was between school periods, and they had about two minutes to head to their next class.

"I woke up this morning, and my ankle felt great. I saw no reason to try to get around anymore with those horrible crutches. In fact, I felt so great that I even rode my bike to school." Mina grinned in triumph.

It was true. She'd woken up and there was zero swelling, and her ankle felt as good as new. She had even tested it by jumping, stretching, and running up and down the stairs to their apartment. It was a small miracle and a blessing at once. Sara had tried to convince Mina to use the crutches per Dr. Martin's orders, but she wouldn't have it. Mina raced outside onto her red Schwinn bike and made it to school in record time. Even Mrs. Porter, her homeroom teacher, wouldn't be able to give her a tardy slip today.

When Mina walked in, she was surprised to see that Coach Potts was at Mrs. Porter's desk. It seemed that the old teacher had retired early and without notice, or that was the rumor going around school. Either way, she was gone, and that meant no more detentions. Mina was ecstatic.

But the day went from great to worse because Jared still hadn't appeared since her glimpse of him at the hospital. Normally, this wouldn't worry Mina because she was kind of used to him showing up whenever he felt like it. She began to worry, though, when Ever, the girl with the spiky hair, approached Mina after school.

"Psst, Gimp!" an irritated voice hissed at her from nowhere.

Mina had only heard one person ever call her "Gimp." She rolled her eyes and turned to see Ever motioning to her from the side of the school.

"What?" Mina asked, annoyed. She walked the fifteen feet to the side of the brick building and they turned the corner, out of the view of most of the students.

Ever's short black hair looked as if it had barely been brushed. Her eyes were wide with fright, and her eyeliner was smeared from crying. Today, she had forgone the skirt and uniform and wore black leggings and a plaid skirt with a denim jacket.

"Have you seen Jared lately?" she mumbled. Her eyes skimmed back and forth nervously at the passing students.

Mina found herself frowning in displeasure at the mention of Jared's name. "No, and I'm not his babysitter," she retorted. She was angry, angry that this girl would call her an ugly name she didn't even know the meaning of. Angrier still that she expected Mina to help her. Mina turned to leave.

Chanda Hahn

Ever, looking distraught, reached out without thinking and grabbed Mina's arm. "I haven't heard from him, or seen him, in over a week. That's not like him."

Mina gave her an appalled look and pulled her arm out of her grasp. "No, that sounds just like the Jared I know. Coming and going whenever he wants. Only thinking of himself. Yep, that's exactly like Jared."

Ever became furious; her hands clenched angrily at her sides. Mina could see that this girl truly hated her.

"That is nothing like Jared. Once he's been called, he always makes sure to try and check in with me every few days. It's our safety system."

"Then you would know if he's okay better than I would," Mina snapped back. "I would actually be quite happy if I never saw him again."

Ever gasped, "Don't say that! You Gimps have no idea what, or who, you are messing with. It's why I hate all of you."

"That's it!" Mina rushed forward angrily and surprised Ever until she backed up into a hard brick school wall. "Why do you keep calling me a Gimp? It's extremely rude. If you want me to help you, you had better explain, and explain now." Mina knew the only reason she had been able to surprise Ever was because she was too distraught over Jared.

Ever recovered quickly, and a wry smile sprouted on her face. "Why, I thought you knew? It's what we Fae call all you stupid and dumb Grimms."

The anger dropped from Mina's face. "You're Fae?" She should have known. Why didn't she? Of course, since Jared was Fae, he probably knew a lot of Fae. They probably banded together and formed their own gang. What Ever said about checking in made sense now. But not why the young Fae thought that Mina would know where he was.

Ever stepped away from the brick wall and stood a little taller. Her chin rose defiantly as she walked into the sunlight. Mina could almost see the faint glow that surrounded her, and when Ever turned a quarter turn to the right and exposed her back, she could see them.

Beautiful pearlescent wings in hues of deep purple and blue sprouted from Ever's back. They were pointed and more jagged than what Mina would have thought fairy wings looked like, but they suited Ever's sharp personality. The girl closed her eyes and moved out of the sunlight; with a moment of concentration, she made her wings disappear.

"You're a fairy?" Mina asked in disbelief.

"Gah! Stars NO! They are happy, twittery, no-brained saps. I'm a pixie," she said rudely.

"I wouldn't have thought ogres and pixies would get along," Mina wondered aloud.

"Ogres!" Ever scoffed. "No, ogres and pixies are mortal enemies. They like to pull our wings off and eat them like candy. Gross! No, I would never go near an ogre."

This new information stunned Mina. How did this Fae not know Jared's true form? She wanted to ask but was interrupted by the perturbed pixie.

"It's been really nice chatting with you, doing the whole girl-talk thing, but I'm over it now. Are you going to let me talk to Jared or what?"

Mina shifted uncomfortably under her stare. "Uh, yeah, sure. You have my permission to talk to him whenever you want. And when you see him, tell him thanks for ditching me in the forest."

The color drained from Ever's face. "That's not funny, Mina." It was the first time the girl had ever said her name.

"Look, Ever. I don't know what kind of relationship you think Jared and I have, but it isn't a close one. I can't help you." Mina turned and pulled her backpack over her shoulder.

"No, wait. I'm sorry." Ever looked distraught again and stared down at her black boots, rubbing the toe against the gravel. She took a deep breath and looked at Mina, her eyes belaying the insecurities she refused to speak. "I'm sorry that I called you a Gimp and was rude to you. It's just part of my defense mechanism as being a pixie. We are kind of low on the food chain, you know."

Mina blinked in surprise. "Um, apology accepted."

Ever let out a sigh of relief. "Good, I'm glad. Now, if you can just check and see..."

"Ever," Mina breathed out her name in exasperation. "I've already told you — I don't know where Jared is. I can't check and see if I don't know where he is."

"But you called him! He came to you when you called him." The poor girl was confused.

"No, I never called him. I don't even know his phone number." Mina was done with this conversation. She now realized that maybe it wasn't the Grimms who were dumb, but the Fae.

In an instant, the contrite and sorry Ever was replaced by a very loud and angry pixie. Her voice rose in anger, and her eyes darkened in power. Mina could feel a cold breeze set in, and the wind picked up leaves from the ground and swirled them around Ever angrily. It took a moment for Mina to realize the girl was beating her invisible wings in anger.

"You Gimp! You lost it, didn't you? How could you do something so stupid, so careless?"

"What are you talking about?" Mina called out, but Ever had turned her back on her and pulled something out of her pocket that looked like a silver lipstick tube.

Ever opened the tube and began to draw a large human-sized oval in the sky. The silver tube sparked and zapped, and a shimmering line appeared where Ever drew. Seconds later, the oval began to glow, and the school lawn disappeared, to be replaced by a door of light.

"Ever, what is that? What are you doing?" Mina held up her hand to block the blinding light that poured through the door. She could vaguely see outlines of silver and white trees on the other side.

"You lost the Grimoire, stupid! Someone needs to tell the Queen before all hell breaks loose and something bad happens." She moved toward the door of light and turned before stepping through to shoot one last remark at Mina.

"I always knew that of all the Grimms, you would cause the most trouble. I told him you didn't deserve the Grimoire. I knew you were a mistake right from the beginning, and I was right."

She stepped through the gate of light, and both Ever and the doorway to the Fae plane disappeared, leaving Mina to wonder what she meant by something bad happening.

CHAPTER 16

The car ride to Nan's party was boring and uneventful. Sara continually tried to console Mina about the loss of the Grimoire, but it didn't help. Sara turned off the highway and drove their green four-door Subaru wagon onto a barely visible dirt road.

"Are you sure these are the right directions?" she asked Mina.

Mina pulled out the wadded-up notebook paper and checked it again for the eighth time. "Yes, we take the interstate southbound for thirty miles. Hang a right at Carl's Junction and left at Anawatchie Road. Drive for four miles and take the first dirt path on your right. Cabin's on the left."

The dirt road narrowed even further down the hill, and they came to a sharp left turn, followed by a metal bridge. One look told Mina that this road was barely wide enough for two cars side by side or a small Subaru. Sara wisely slowed their car, opened the window, and listened for the sound of oncoming cars before pushing on the gas and crossing the bridge at a faster pace than she would normally drive.

"Boy, I would not want to be driving this route during the winter." Sara chuckled nervously.

"Well, you won't have to, because the cabin is closed during the winter." Mina wasn't in the most congenial of moods. In fact, she was downright sour. Haunted by Ever's parting words, Mina found little rest or comfort without the Grimoire. Panicking, she had run back to the hospital; spoken to numerous nurses, doctors, staff; and dug through their lost and found — nothing. No one had seen her notebook.

Sara had tried to be comforting about the loss, but she was just as worried as her daughter. She made daily trips to the hospital looking for it. Finally, they both decided it must have been lost in the woods. There was no other explanation. Mina tried to remember the last time she had it, and all she could recall was that it was somewhere between the bear attack and the hospital. The signs were not good of her ever finding it.

The only solace she could give herself was that her Uncle Jack had never had the Grimoire, and he had been successful at completing some of the Fae tales. So she would just have to be smarter and more resourceful than her Uncle Jack, who was dead. Yeah, Mina knew she was in serious trouble.

"I know you have a lot on your mind, sweetie," Sara said softly to Mina. "But everything will be okay. It has to be." She reached over carefully, keeping her eyes on the road, to brush her daughter's soft brown hair.

What Sara didn't understand was the real cause for Mina's attitude. Even though they were in the car, being surrounded by woods on all sides was really messing with Mina's mind. She had a hard time breathing and focusing without having flashbacks to being abandoned in the woods. Luckily, the road widened again, and they could see a beautiful crystal-blue lake in the distance and a very large three-story cedar house.

This wasn't a small wooden cabin like Mina had pictured. It was a huge rustic hunting lodge in the middle of nowhere. Mina could see as they drove closer that they weren't the first to arrive at the party. In fact, it looked like they were the last, as at least twenty cars could be seen parked along the driveway in the grass. Lots of her classmates were already in swimsuits and diving off a small wooden dock on the lake. Many were hanging out by a very classy stone fire pit; others played sand volleyball.

They passed a very familiar black SUV, and Mina felt her heart flutter in nervousness. Brody was already here. Mina did her best to compose herself and felt a little embarrassed to be dropped off at the party by her mom and little brother.

"I'll pick you up tomorrow evening. Be sure to have fun," Sara called out as Mina closed the car door. She gripped her duffle bag with her extra clothes for the weekend, thankful that no one else was spending the night. Her embarrassment became monumentally worse when Sara turned the car around and did their family tradition of saying goodbye by doing a double horn beep and wave.

When Mina's family drove away and she could no longer see the taillights of her mom's car, she finally gathered enough courage to make her way toward the nearest cluster of laughing students. Unfortunately, the closest groups of girls happened to include Savannah White and Priscilla Rose. Mina felt her hackles rise in annoyance when Savannah verbally made fun of her.

"Aw, how sweet, Grimey, that your mommy drove you here. Does she still make your bed and pack your lunch for you, too?" Savannah laughed obnoxiously at her own joke. The queen of white-blonde curls, though horrible, still looked amazing in red shorts and a white-striped distressed T-shirt and sandals.

"Uh, no, Savannah, she only drives me when the chauffeur has the day off," Mina snapped back, feeling surprised at her own outburst. But it wasn't long before the group began firing other comments back. She gritted her teeth and kept walking, ignoring both Savannah and her groupies. But where else should she go? She saw Steve and Frank down by the lake trying to push each other in; the mock fight was over when both boys ended up in the lake. She supposed Nan had to be at the house, so she decided to start her search there.

The path to the house was marked with stone steps and lined with gardenias. A beautiful porch wrapped around the whole house, offering rockers, benches, and the occasional swing. She decided to follow the porch around to the back of the house, where she found another outdoor seating area with blankets and an expensive outdoor fireplace. Mina was secretly envious, and she hadn't even been inside yet. Entering through the back led Mina right to the heart of the house, the kitchen.

The kitchen had the latest state-of-the-art appliances, granite countertops, three separate ovens, an indoor grill, and a huge island. Mina found Nan sitting on the island, talking animatedly to two students.

"Mina, good, you're finally here. Look who came." Nan motioned toward her company, and Mina stopped when she immediately recognized one of them. It was Brody with a girl. No, wait, that wasn't a girl with short blonde hair. It was Valdemar, Brody's cousin.

Both Brody and Valdemar turned to greet her. Brody quickly looked away, barely making eye contact. Valdemar walked over and gave Mina a warm welcome like they were long-lost friends.

"Good to see you, Nina." He opened his arms wide and pulled her into a quick and awkward hug.

"Good to see you again, Valdemar, and it's Mina," she corrected.

"That's what I said, lass. You mustn't have heard me right. And tonight, just call me Peter." He backed up a step and leaned against the island, pressing a shoulder accidentally against Nan. Her cheeks burned red, and her eyes flickered toward Valdemar/Peter and quickly away.

Brody nodded his head in greeting, meeting her eyes with the barest hint of a question burning behind them. She knew without a doubt that he was going to approach her tonight and talk to her. She turned and looked over the table full of snacks and drinks; she had seen another table just like this filled with food outside as well. Nan's mom and Dr. Martin really knew how to throw a party. Mina wondered briefly where they were, until the roar of a boat engine revving to life drew her attention out the window toward the lake.

There Dr. Martin and Veronica could be seen taking a group of kids out onto the lake in his speed boat. She watched in fascination as the four teens, wearing bright orange life jackets, screamed in excitement when he steered to the middle of the lake and hit the throttle. They quickly became little bouncing balls of orange as they skittered across the lake at breakneck speed.

Briefly, Mina wondered why Nan wasn't out there enjoying the boat ride, until she remembered her famous company. Nan was hiding out in the kitchen, trying to keep Peter all to herself. She knew that once everyone else saw him the partygoers would quickly congregate to wherever he was, which also meant that she was probably going to hide him from most of her guests for as long as possible. Mina had no idea how Nan was going to accomplish keeping his anonymity; she was just glad that she didn't have to do it.

Brody followed Mina to the snack table and began to fill up a paper plate with small, rectangular sandwich bites. Mina grabbed a two-liter bottle of Coke and had begun to fill her own blue plastic cup with the bubbly goodness when Nan caught her off guard.

"Mina, have you seen Jared lately? I invited him, but I haven't seen him at school." Nan spoke innocently enough, but the question spooked Mina and she lost control of the bottle, dropping it into her cup and flipping both onto the floor. The two-liter rolled under the table, spilling soda in its wake.

"Stink!" Mina dropped to her knees and raced under the table to upright the bottle. With a pile of napkins, she haphazardly began to mop up the spilled mess. It wasn't even close to enough napkins.

Brody ducked under the table and handed her another stack of napkins. With his own stack, he began to help clean up the quickly spreading puddle. Her hands shook in embarrassment; she could feel her cheeks and neck burning. She stopped mopping to glance at him. He wore a blue shirt, which complemented his eyes, and in quarters this close she could smell his cologne. He must have sensed her staring at him, because he looked right at her and smiled out of the corner of his mouth.

Mortified at being caught staring, Mina jumped up but bashed her head on the underside of the table, making it move three inches to the right.

It didn't matter how much of a gentleman he was, no one could see that and not laugh.

He chuckled at her clumsiness when she plopped right back down into her soppy napkin and soda mess. "Are you all right?" he asked, trying to mask his own laughter.

Mina clutched her head and shot dagger-filled looks of hate at the table. "No, I doubt I will ever be classified as 'all right.'"

The table moved above her as Nan and Peter shifted the heavy oak table away. Nan had found a mop, and Peter had retrieved a large roll of paper towels. Between the two of them, they cleaned up Mina's mess in record time.

There were no words to describe her humiliation at having Brody and his rock star cousin cleaning up her mess.

What was worse was that Mina was now soaked in brown soda. It had spilled all over her shirt and shorts. She was on the verge of crying when Nan came to the rescue again.

"Hey," she whispered, grabbing Mina's hand and pulling her to the side. "Go upstairs, and the first door on the right is the guest room. It's where you will be sleeping tonight. You brought extra clothes, right? Then just go change and throw your clothes in the upstairs washer." She patted Mina encouragingly on the shoulder and nudged her toward the stairs.

Slowly she trudged up the stairs. Her feet felt like lead as her own worries and anxiety weighed her down emotionally. She found the bedroom and opened her backpack to grab the first pair of shorts and shirt she found. Not even caring if they matched, she slowly walked into the bathroom to rinse out her clothes and change. Her movements became sluggish as she tried to delay her return to the kitchen.

In a house filled with people, she felt completely alone. When she had cleaned her clothes as much as possible, Mina wiped her hands on a soft hand towel, gathering the courage to look into the bathroom mirror and inspect her eye makeup. Only it wasn't her soft brown eyes looking back at her in the mirror. They were someone else's, and they were angry.

CHAPTER 17

Mina screamed. She leapt away from the bathroom sink and crashed into the wall, her mouth open wide in terror as she tried to process what she was seeing. She could barely see her reflection in the bathroom mirror because it was faded in comparison to the other reflection coming through the mirror. She recognized those grey eyes. They were Jared's. Once again, she was seeing his reflection.

He was angry and yelling at her. She couldn't hear him, but she only needed to read his facial expressions and lips. He ran his hands through his dark hair in frustration, turned and pointed at her again, and continued yelling.

Mina shrugged in response and pointed to her ears, pantomiming she couldn't hear him. Jared cursed, or at least she thought he did. Clenching his fist, he slammed it against the mirror over and over in frustration and desperation. She saw the mirror twitch a little each time he hit it, or maybe she just imagined it. But either way, it looked like Jared was trapped in the mirror.

Jared became still and walked toward the glass. He leaned forward, bringing his mouth close to the other side of the mirror. Taking a deep breath, he slowly breathed warm air onto the invisible barrier, leaving a large circle of condensation. Quickly, he reached out one finger and began to write furiously backward.

The words appeared on Mina's side, simple and short: HELP ME!

She reached out to touch the words and felt the coolness of the condensation on her side of the mirror. How was that possible? She touched the mirror and left a small fingerprint in the disappearing condensation. Whatever he was doing was moving through the mirror and having an effect on her side. Mina imitated Jared's actions and breathed on the mirror. She watched as his eyes widened in hope.

She took her finger and drew three letters. HOW? But she forgot to write them backward, so it looked like "WOH" to Jared. He quickly read the letters, and his shoulders dropped in disappointment. Obviously, he didn't know the answer and was hoping she did. He took a step away from the mirror into the darkness that was surrounding him. He was leaving!

"NO!" Mina yelled. "Don't give up!" Desperately she grabbed the first thing her hand rested on, a bronze vase. She climbed onto the countertop and raised the vase over her head to bring it down.

Jared saw her actions and began to violently shake his head no and wave his arms, but it was too late. The vase connected with the mirror, shattering it. The force of the blow brought the frame down with it.

Mina stared at where the mirror had hung and was confused by the plain blank wall behind it. She looked around at the shards of mirror on the floor and didn't see a single reflection of Jared in any of them. She put the vase back down on the counter and stepped back to the floor. Letting her back slide against the cupboards, she sank into the mess of glass. Not caring about her scratched and bleeding hands, she picked up a piece of the mirror and called Jared's name. Nothing. He didn't appear. He was gone.

Footsteps sounded loudly on the stairs, and the bathroom door flew open. Dr. Martin came into the bathroom and wrestled the piece of glass out of her hands. Mina argued with him and tried to get it back.

"Stop it!" he commanded angrily. "I will not let you harm yourself. Do you understand? I don't care what happened — it is no reason to take your own life." He reached for a towel and pressed it against the cut across her palm.

Mina stilled at his words. He thought she had broken the mirror and was trying to commit suicide. It was completely absurd, but she couldn't argue when the evidence spoke against her.

"No, it's not what it looks like! I wasn't trying to — I don't know how to explain — I wasn't..." She bit her lip when he pulled open a drawer and poured peroxide on the cut. He began to wrap the wound with bandages from the same drawer. She had to hand it to him; the good doctor sure did keep his supplies stocked.

He paused and looked at her carefully. "Then try to explain what happened here. Otherwise, I'm calling your mom, and you are going home. I don't care if you are Nan's best friend. I don't want her hanging out with someone that is a bad influence." On the word "influence," he pulled the bandage a little too tight, and her leg flinched. She thumped her head against the bathroom cabinet in sudden surprise from the pain.

"Ow!" she mumbled, rubbing her head carefully. "Would you believe that I am just that clumsy?"

"Then what was with the glass?" He held the piece of mirror that he had taken from her; it still had a few specks of blood on it. But it gave Mina the proof she needed.

"It's only spots of blood. I was washing my hands when the mirror detached from the wall and fell on me. I used my hands to protect my head when it fell. Look around. Other than a few scratches from the glass on the outside of my arms, I have no injuries. I cut the inside of my palm when I tried to clean up the mess. That's when you came in."

She held out her arms, exposing her wrists and flipping them to show the back of her hands. "All the damage is on the back of my hands. Proof I wasn't trying to hurt myself. You have to believe me when I say I am extremely clumsy and have inherent bad luck."

"Hmm," he intoned, before slowly regarding the bathroom and broken mirror thoughtfully.

"Where's Nan?" Mina asked quickly before he accused her of anything else.

Dr. Martin didn't look at her; he continued to scrutinize the wall where the mirror had hung earlier. She could tell he was weighing the possibilities, still deciding if he was going to believe her. "Out on the dock with Veronica — they're getting ready for a boat ride."

"Oh," Mina moaned sadly. She was surprised that her best friend had left the house without telling her. It was obvious Nan had forgotten about her; she was preoccupied.

"Come on," he mumbled and pulled her up to her feet. "She wouldn't let Veronica take off without you. It's getting dark soon, and then we have to light the bonfire."

Her spirits lifted instantly.

He held stubbornly onto her shoulder when she tried to move away. She looked at him, and he spoke quietly, barely above a whisper. "I don't believe you're telling me the whole truth, but I want you to know that I love Veronica and her daughter like my own. If you do anything to influence Nan or cause her harm, there will be serious consequences."

"I understand, but let me — " Mina started.

Dr. Martin held up his hand, cutting her off. "This conversation is over." He held the door open and waited for Mina to pass through it first. She couldn't help but pick up her pace and practically ran down the stairs out of the house, feeling duly chastised and ashamed.

She ran past the students gathering by the bonfire and felt the sting of tears. She would not cry. It was stupid to cry.

Veronica waved at Mina when she made it to the dock. "There you are, sweetie. We were worried about you," Veronica called out kindly; her long blonde hair was braided into a single plait over her shoulder. With the excitement of being on the speedboat making her cheeks flushed, she looked very much like Nan at the moment. Nan, on the other hand, was sitting on the bench wearing a red polka-dot swimsuit and engaged with every word Peter spoke.

But it was just the two young people with Veronica; Brody wasn't on the boat. Mina wasn't sure why, but she had assumed he would take the boat ride with them. She turned and scanned the dock and saw Brody by the unlit bonfire with Savannah and Pri. Dr. Martin had just joined them by the bonfire and was arranging the kindling to get it started.

Mina was about to change her mind and get off the boat, but Veronica started the engine and backed away from the dock. It was too late. *Great*, Mina thought wryly. Now she was going to be stuck on a boat ride with two love birds. How awkward. She desperately wished she was back on dry land. The ride would be beautiful; the sun was setting and was the perfect backdrop to a magically romantic evening for Nan and Peter. Mina could see how awestruck Nan was by Peter, and he seemed to be equally entranced with Nan.

The two of them were holding hands, and he was whispering into her ear, neither one of them paying any attention to the inspiring sunset. When they had pulled far enough away from land, Veronica took the boat as fast as it could. Circling back around the lake, riding the crests of their previous waves, the boat would lift off the water over and over.

Nan and Peter screamed in excitement, holding their hands above their heads in triumph, similar to riding a roller coaster. Mina held on to the seat and hated every minute of it. She hated her circumstances, her lot in life, and was even beginning to hate Nan's absolute luck with finding a boyfriend. Mina thought the second time around would be easier for her and Brody to start over, but it was proving even more difficult. She felt her fingernails dig into the leather seat angrily.

It wasn't fair. What was different this time? Was it because she wasn't rich? Or maybe it was because she wasn't pretty enough. Why couldn't she have been born rich or with Nan's good looks? She heard Nan laugh out loud, and it made her cringe in annoyance. The boat ride was becoming torture. She couldn't even look at her best friend without feeling anger, regret for even coming, and a twinge of jealousy. Nan had it so easy; she just happened to sit next to a rock star and get accidentally kissed in a spur-of-the-moment incident, and now she had a boyfriend. She was free to live her life without the threat of a family curse over her head. Free to argue with her parents over which college to attend when Mina didn't even know if she would live long enough to go to college. Free to date anyone without fear of being attacked by the Fae.

The feelings of dissatisfaction and jealousy hit her like a painful stab in the stomach, and Mina felt like she was going to be sick. She motioned to Veronica, who saw how green Mina had become and turned the boat toward the dock.

"Why are we going in?" Nan asked, confused.

Veronica called back over her shoulder, "Mina is going to be sick. I think we've had enough for the night. It's time to get back for the s'mores anyway." She managed to bring the boat around, cut the motor easily, and glide in the rest of the way to the dock.

Nan was visibly upset and kept casting Mina accusing glances. Mina didn't need to wonder what those looks meant. Since they had been best friends for years, she knew that Nan blamed Mina for robbing her of her alone time with Peter. What could she say except that Mina didn't really care? As soon as Dr. Martin ran down the dock to help tie up the boat, Mina was off the boat and up the dock in a split second.

She wanted to get away, to go home. This was not how she pictured the night turning out. But when Mina passed the bonfire, it was impossible to miss the three new latecomers that had arrived. Especially when one had spiked skunk-like hair, and they made enough noise to raise the dead. The rest of the members of the Dead Prince Society were there, and the party really seemed to be getting underway.

Music was blasting. Magnus was once again eating his way through the food on the picnic table. Naga had found extension cords, run them from the house, and hooked up their amplifiers to their guitars. Constantine had brought out his bass for an impromptu music jam. The students were screaming and crowding the band; Naga and Constantine were standing on a table shredding and making a lot of noise that to them was music.

Mina stood off in the distance, watching with mixed emotions. Nan and Peter ran up the dock to greet them excitedly. Dr. Martin pulled Nan aside and waved his hands angrily, obviously upset at the party crashers. Mina could see Nan throw her hands on her hips and yell back. Veronica came to her daughter's rescue, and the argument came to a close. Dr. Martin shook his head in annoyance and stormed off into the house. Veronica and her daughter rushed over to the tables and watched as Peter joined his band mates in the impromptu concert. Instantly, his persona changed, and he was once again Valdemar.

Brody was right up front, jumping and singing along with Nan. Mina felt utterly alone and forgotten. What had happened to this night? It was supposed to be fun, and now she felt like an outcast. She hated it here. Anger stirred in her, and Mina grabbed a bunch of grapes off the nearest table and pulled one off to chuck at a tree. No one noticed except for Magnus, who mumbled something about wasting food. He didn't seem inclined to join his band mates in the merrymaking. Everyone else was distracted by the concert. Feeling only slightly appeased by the sudden release of energy gained by throwing the food, she grabbed another item and tossed it again. Angrily, she began to throw grape after grape, aiming for a tree, imagining it was Savannah White. It felt good to throw food at her imaginary enemy. But soon her target had Nan's smiling face on it.

Not feeling at all surprised by the direction her mind was taking, Mina reached for something bigger to throw. She gripped the large projectile, took aim, and was about to release it when a hand reached out and stopped her wrist mid-throw, the red apple still clutched in her palm.

Magnus grabbed her wrist and pulled the apple from her hand. Although he was strong, he didn't hurt her. "Don't let your jealousy and anger rule your emotions," he said in a soft voice. "Nothing good will ever come of it." He raised the apple to his own mouth and took a bite. The soft crunch of apple between his teeth made Mina reflect on what she was doing. It didn't have the intended effect. Instead of feeling ashamed, she felt more anger.

"You know nothing about what I'm feeling or thinking. No one knows what I'm going through. So don't go all Dalai Lama on me." She stormed off toward the house, breathing hard from her resentment.

She felt the tingle of power begin to gather around her when she reached the front porch. Normally, feeling the power of the Story would make her scared. This time she was too angry to care. She turned toward the bonfire. The light from the fire illuminated the happy, smiling faces of the students as they partied, danced, and sang. She could see them all: Brody, Savannah, T.J., Frank, Steve, Pri, and the others, but her focus drifted toward Nan and stayed there. How could her friend be so oblivious? She was so enraptured in her new guy that she was ignoring her best friend. At that moment, Mina was filled with resentment toward them all and jealousy toward her friend.

"I wish it would rain," Mina mumbled under her breath. "Then they would all leave, and I could have my best friend back."

Instantly, static raced through her fingers, and she felt it through every inch of her body. It made the hair on the back of her arms stand on end. Clouds formed out of nothing, covering the stars and the moon. The breeze shifted on the lake, bringing a cold northern wind. The smell that precedes a thunderstorm penetrated the air, followed by a crack of thunder.

Students screamed in fright. They looked up as another crack of lightning arced across the sky. Immediately, the band unplugged their instruments as the first droplets of water began to pour down on the crowd. In seconds, everyone was drenched. Mina watched, feeling somewhat smug as Savannah raced for cover and reached the porch looking like a sopping mess. Most of the students raced for the covered porch: others, for their cars. When the storm didn't let up, the majority of the students went home. Not even being in the welcoming lodge appeased the teenagers wearing water-logged shoes and clothes.

Mina stayed away from everyone, scared and exhilarated at what had happened. Had she just manipulated the power of the Story into creating a storm? It sure felt like it, but why? Why would she have the power to control the weather, especially when she didn't have the Grimoire? It gave her plenty to think about. She smiled somewhat slyly and headed up to her guest room. She didn't want to spend any more time with Nan and her boyfriend, and Brody hadn't made a single move to speak to her.

She locked the door and sat on the edge of the bed, looking out the window. Her window overlooked the front yard of the house and had a fantastic view of Imperial Lake. An hour later, she heard a car pull up, and Mina stood up and walked solemnly over to the window. She wasn't sure why, but something deep down inside her spoke to her, told her to look. To look at what was happening underneath her very nose.

She pressed close to the glass and saw Brody's SUV pull up to the porch, windshield wipers on high, battling the torrential rain that was still falling. Music poured out of the car, and she could see the overhead light inside as he opened the passenger door for someone who dashed into the front seat. He spoke a few words to the passenger and then closed the door. The car went dark for a second as Brody raced around to the driver's-side door. When he opened up his door, the car was illuminated once again, and Mina could see who his passenger was. It was Nan.

Mina didn't see anything else as she stepped back away from the window. Her hand reached for her heart as it exploded with the pain of betrayal. How could she? How could she go off with Brody, at night and alone? She knew that Mina liked him. Only hours ago she was all snuggled up with Peter. How could her best friend do this?

In her irrational state of mind, the only conclusion she could reach was that Nan never cared about Mina at all. It was all an act. She only cared about using her to get to Brody. Images of them singing in the car, laughing together, texting each other about her birthday played in her mind. It made sense.

She heard gravel kick up as the SUV pulled away. Mina raced back to the window and watched as they pulled away down the road. Mina cried silently, her tears mingling with the rain as it washed down the glass window. She moved from the window and collapsed on the bed.

"Please, make it stop," she cried to no one in particular. "Make the pain stop. I don't want to feel this way. Make it stop!" She was too focused on her own pain to see Jared's form appear faintly in the window, trying to warn her. He was shaking his head violently.

"I just want this feeling to go away. I don't want to hurt anymore. Make it stop." Mina never meant for anyone to hear her pain, but someone heard, someone listened. Mina finally cried herself to sleep, unaware of the rustle of wind that picked up in her room, moving her hair slightly by some unseen force.

She was awakened later by the sirens of a police car. Her room was awash in the rotating colors of blue and red. She raced to the window to see two police cars pulled up outside. It had quit raining, and Dr. Martin and Veronica were on the gravel driveway speaking to two officers in uniform.

Mina couldn't hear what was going on but could tell something bad had happened. The police officer was pointing down the road to where Brody and Nan had driven earlier. Veronica screamed, crumpled to the ground, and began sobbing loudly. Dr. Martin held his fiancée and whispered softly to her, rocking her. He held Veronica close to him, and he looked up at the sky, silent tears flowing down his face. She stepped back in horror; her heart raced as she stared out the glass. Slowly smog began to form on the window pane, creating a vision in slow motion, and she could see it all.

It came rushing forward, images flashing in front of her on the glass, as if she were there in the car. The downpour had washed away most of the road on the dangerous curve, and Brody, not knowing it was gone, took the curve too fast. The car slipped down the embankment and rolled over and over. She could hear Nan screaming and Brody trying to reach over and protect Nan. The car came to a stop in a sudden collision with a tree at the bottom of the ditch. She could see them clear as day.

Brody groaned, blood pouring out of a gash on his forehead from hitting the steering wheel. He reached over to Nan, but she didn't respond. He shook her arm slightly, but nothing. He began to yell loudly, although Mina couldn't hear what he said through the glass vision. He pulled his seatbelt off and reached for her neck to check for a pulse. She saw him look through the wreckage of his car to find his cell phone. He dialed 911. He spoke quickly and urgently to the operator, and Mina watched his lips carefully. She fell to the floor in shock and couldn't breathe.

It couldn't be true! She looked back up to the fogged window pane, and in slow motion it played Brody's last words to the operator, over and over. She could easily make them out.

"She's dead."

CHAPTER 18

Mina flew down the stairs, knocking over a table lamp at the bottom in her rush to leave the house. The door crashed open, and Mina ran past a sobbing Veronica and a stunned Dr. Martin. The police officers yelled something unintelligible after her, but she didn't stop to listen. Her heart pounded in her chest, and her shoes slid in the mud as she ran down the road. It wasn't far before she saw the lights of more police cars, ambulances, and fire trucks about a quarter mile away.

This was all her fault! She knew it deep down. Somehow the Story must have heard her thoughts and wishes, but this wasn't the outcome she wanted. She never wanted to hurt anyone, especially the two people she cared about most.

She was crying hysterically and had problems seeing in the dark. If she went straight through the woods downhill, she could cut her distance in half instead of following the curving road. Not caring about how many scratches or cuts she got, Mina fell, tumbled, and slid on her bottom down the long hill. The forest took on an eerie appearance, since it was illuminated by the red, blue, and white lights of the emergency vehicles. A loud whirring sound echoed through the night, and sparks illuminated the forest. The firefighters were cutting Nan out of the car, so the paramedics hadn't been able to reach her yet. Maybe her vision was wrong, and she was still alive.

"Nan! Brody!" Mina screamed, and continued her descent. "I'm sorry," she chanted over and over as she stepped over a fallen tree. "I'll save you!" She pushed a tree limb out of the way and continued, praying the whole way.

A rush of tingling sensations overwhelmed Mina, and she saw a large electric oval of sparks appear. She had seen a circle like this appear once before, and that was when Ever created a doorway to the Fae plane. Now something on the Fae plane was coming through here.

Mina backed up and away from the sparkling doorway to take refuge behind a tree. She clamped a hand over her mouth to slow her breathing, too scared to look at what could be coming through. She had a fifty-fifty chance of it being either a good Fae or a bad Fae. Either way, without the Grimoire, she was just a normal sixteen-year-old girl.

The glow became brighter and brighter. She wondered if the police officers down the hill would notice the ethereal light, or if they were too preoccupied with their rescue. She didn't even know if Brody had made it out of the car yet.

The forest darkened for a second as whatever was coming over passed through the gate and blocked the light from the Fae world. The woods filled with the scent of freshly cut gardenias. A second later, the forest went completely dark again. Now Mina was in the woods alone with a Fae. She closed her eyes and listened for sounds of movement. If she screamed, someone would come running…she hoped. That was, if they heard her over the sound of the jaws of life

There it was, the sound of leaves crunching. Someone was walking toward her behind the tree. She was going to die, she knew it. But at least she wasn't going to die without a fight. Quietly, Mina slid down the tree and reached for a stick that was by her foot. If she got the jump on the creature from the Fae plane, she might be able to immobilize it.

She gripped the stick, took a deep breath, mentally counted to three, and sprang from behind the tree, stick held high. She froze at the sight of what was in front of her.

An ethereal woman, pale, hair like starlight, wrapped in the bluest silk, stood before her, a crown of silver stood upon her brow. She looked upon the stick that Mina held up in the air as a weapon. Her beautiful brow arched high in disbelief. She flicked a finger, and the stick flew from Mina's hands to land somewhere in the forest behind her.

"Who are you?" Mina asked, somewhat in awe and somewhat fearful.

"I am Maeve, and I have come to make a bargain with you," she said simply, without emotion.

Mina looked over the woman carefully. She knew better than to make bargains with the Fae. She shook her head, but the Fae woman raised one finger carefully. Mina felt her head immediately stop shaking. She no longer controlled her own body.

"I would be careful before answering without hearing my terms. Once a bargain has been made, it cannot be undone." She stretched her pale white hand and pointed with a polished finger toward the wrecked car and the emergency team, working hard on rescuing her friends. Mina could see car lights coming down road from the lodge and had to assume it was Dr. Martin and Veronica.

"Okay," Mina whispered nervously. "Let me hear your terms. But I'm warning you, if you are trying to delay me from saving my friends, then I will hear none of it."

Maeve lowered her arm and closed her eyes, and a slight glow appeared around the beautiful Fae woman. She opened her eyes and spoke without emotion. "The girl is already dead. The boy has a slight concussion but will live."

"You lie!" Mina argued, sliding to her knees in the dirt of the forest. "Nan can't be dead. It can't be true."

"But it is, my child. You've failed your quest, and failed in your duties as the keeper of the Grimoire," Maeve answered. "But I can give you hope, if you agree to my bargain."

Mina stiffened at Maeve's words. "My mother told me never to trust the Fae."

"Then your friend is lost for all eternity." The Fae queen spoke firmly; her eyes glowing in anger. She turned, and, reaching her hand into her dress, she pulled out a silver tube to create the doorway to leave.

"Wait, what is it that you want?" Mina was desperate, willing to do anything if it could bring Nan back.

Maeve turned around and stared at Mina. It was easy to see that she was starting to lose her hold on her emotions. "I will make you a bargain that has never been offered to a Grimm before, but never before has a Grimm made such a grave error and done the unthinkable."

"You mean lose the Grimoire," Mina answered angrily. "I would think that would make you happy, seeing that it makes it almost impossible for me to complete my quests."

Maeve's eyes flared and a cold wind blew, whipping Mina's hair around her face. "Silence, you insignificant human. Your ignorance is costing innocent Fae their lives. The Grimoire is a prison. It is being used to trap Fae within its pages."

Mina felt slighted, and her anger rose to match Maeve's. "Yes, I know all of that. Jared explained it to me. He also told me that you and the Story manipulate the quests so that the Grimms trap your enemies for you. You use me and my family to do your dirty work. And we have died doing it."

The wind quit attacking Mina as Maeve calmed down. "Yes, when a queen is cornered, she must sacrifice pawns to protect her king."

The chessboard analogy made Mina pause in thought. Someone else had spoken similar words, but at the moment she couldn't remember who.

"The Grimoire has fallen into the hands of an enemy. I know not who, but they are using the Grimoire to trap innocent Fae. Even you cannot plead ignorance to these circumstances, because it was you who lost it. And it is you who must pay for those lives that are lost. It is only a matter of time before more disappear. You know of whom I speak, don't you?"

Mina pondered, unsure of what Maeve was talking about, and then it came to her. "You mean the missing people — the UPS delivery guy, the DMV worker, and the coffee girl?"

"Even your teacher," she answered solemnly.

"Mrs. Porter, my homeroom teacher? I thought she just retired?"

Maeve shook her head. "All innocents, all imprisoned unjustly."

"I wouldn't say all are innocent," Mina said out loud, thinking of how cruel Mrs. Porter was to her. But if she were Fae, then it made sense why she hated Mina. She was a Grimm.

Maeve became angry again. "ALL were INNOCENT. All imprisoned because of your mistake, and they are paying the price. Especially my son."

"Your son?" Mina asked, but Maeve ignored her.

"I cannot undo what has been done, but I can change the outcome. The rest is up to you, as long as you promise to find the Grimoire and not lose it again. For it holds that which is most precious to me."

"Do you mean you can save Nan?"

"No, I cannot save her fully, but I can give you a fighting chance to save her. If you are willing."

"YES!" Mina cried out, tears flowing down her face. "I am willing. I will try anything to save her."

"So you agree?" Maeve asked.

"Yes, I agree," Mina answered before she realized she had agreed without understanding the full terms.

Maeve opened her arms and spread them wide. Her eyes glowed with ethereal power. The stars themselves seemed brighter and closer to the earth than what was naturally possible. The leaves rustled and began to swirl in the air around Maeve, starting at her feet and then rising slowly into the air.

"Then you must go!" she whispered to Mina.

"What? Go where?"

"GO!" she ordered.

Mina bolted, ignoring the Fae woman in the woods. She continued running down the hill toward the wreck. She could see that Nan's body had been pulled from the car and was on a stretcher. The paramedics gathered around her pulled away. It was obvious that their attempt to revive her was unsuccessful.

Dr. Martin was holding on to a hysterical Veronica as they slowly lifted the stretcher into the ambulance. There was no longer any hurry, because they couldn't save her. They weren't rushing to the hospital; they were driving her to the morgue.

"NO, WAIT!" Mina cried as she stumbled onto the road, knowing that she probably looked wild-eyed and terrifying. "She's not dead!" A firefighter stopped her from running toward the stretcher, trying to hold her back.

Veronica sobbed even louder at Mina's announcement. Dr. Martin looked at Mina crossly.

"Dr. Martin, you're a doctor. You must believe me, she's not dead," Mina screamed again, and struggled against the man holding her.

Dr. Martin looked disgusted and came over to speak to Mina. "It's because I'm a doctor that I know she is dead. I checked myself. Don't go causing more problems, Mina. I'm warning you," he threatened.

"Dr. Martin, please trust me! She's not dead. Don't give up on her." She kicked the fireman in the shin and ran toward the ambulance. She was so distracted she didn't see the person sitting on the second ambulance bumper until he stood up and blocked her path.

Brody grasped Mina's upper arms and pulled her into a hug. "Don't. Don't upset them more. She was dead over a half hour ago. She was dead before I called the ambulance." He looked down at her, his blue eyes filled with grief and sorrow, his red-rimmed eyes proof that he had been crying for a while.

"No, you're wrong. You don't know her like I do. She's a fighter. She's going to go to Julliard in a couple of years. She is NOT dead!" Mina yelled at Brody.

"Mina." He spoke her name, and his eyes welled up with tears again. "Mina, you have to let her go — she's gone."

"Brody Carmichael, let go of me NOW!" she ordered and shrugged him off angrily. "I can't believe that you won't even try to save her."

Brody looked pained at her words. "I did. I tried everything I could to save her."

Mina raised her chin angrily. "Obviously, it wasn't enough, because you got her killed." She pushed him away and stormed over to Veronica, who was still crying.

"Listen to me. Mrs. Taylor, listen — she's not dead. Don't let them take her to the hospital morgue. Tell them to take her to the emergency room now!"

Veronica was as pale as a ghost; her lips trembled. Her eyes wouldn't focus on Mina, but deep down, Mina knew that the woman could hear her. Mina repeated her command over and over until Veronica nodded in agreement.

She stood up and glared at her boyfriend. "She's right. Don't let them take my baby to the morgue. She's not dead." She pushed Dr. Martin away and opened the back of the ambulance. She crawled in next to the stretcher and her daughter's still form zipped in a black bag. She motioned for Mina to join her in the ambulance.

Ignoring a bewildered Brody and an angry Dr. Martin, she jumped in the ambulance and slid across from Veronica, who was having a very interesting argument with the ambulance driver.

"NO! You take us right to the emergency room right now. You put those fancy lights and horns on now. We have a girl to save."

The EMTs looked over their shoulder at Dr. Martin, who had closed the back door and slid next to his fiancée, for confirmation. He looked warily over at Mina and the stubborn mother fighting a lost cause, and he sighed wearily. "Well, you heard her — go!"

The two paramedics shrugged, hit the lights, and pulled out onto the road toward the hospital.

Mina zipped open the bag and had to stop herself from crying out. There was so much blood across Nan's face, but it was mostly from a head wound. She couldn't see anything that was life-threatening or that was an obvious reason behind her death. It gave Mina hope. She looked around the ambulance, recognized a stethoscope, and handed it to Dr. Martin. "Don't give up," she whispered to him encouragingly.

"We have an electronic heart monitor, Mina," he said dejectedly, already giving up. "They tried to resuscitate her and it didn't work."

Mina shook her head. "Machines can make mistakes. People can make mistakes. Don't listen to this." She pointed to the heart monitor. "Listen to this." Mina reached forward and touched his chest. "What is your heart telling you? Mine is telling me to believe, to have faith."

He took the silver stethoscope while tears poured out of his eyes. He put the plugs in his ears and leaned forward to listen to Nan's lifeless heart. Mina waited with bated breath and prayed. They pulled onto the main highway, and the ambulance picked up speed. Veronica encouraged them to use the siren, and they caught her urgency.

Minutes ticked by with nothing. *What is going on?* Mina thought. Maeve promised that she was going to save Nan's life. Dr. Martin took down the hand pump and put it over Nan's mouth and nose. He adjusted the knob on the air tank and started her on the artificial breathing; he listened to her heart and then began the chest compressions. There were no obvious signs of life coming from her, so he continued the basics of lifesaving CPR. The ambulance turned off the highway and onto the main road to the hospital. Still there were no signs from Nan.

"Come on, baby," Veronica whispered, holding her daughter's hand between hers. "Come on, baby, breathe."

"You can do it, Nan," Dr. Martin coaxed. "Do it for your mom and me." He continued the chest compressions, but after another thirty seconds Mina could see the defeat in his eyes.

Mina began to cry again as the ambulance turned into the hospital and headed for the emergency entrance. This wasn't part of the deal. This wasn't how it was supposed to end.

Dr. Martin reached for the stethoscope to take it off, but Veronica grabbed his hands, desperation ringing in her voice. "Please, Robert, listen one more time."

He hung his head, afraid to look at her, but he did it. He leaned down, placed the metal circle over Nan's heart, and listened.

Mina and Veronica held their breath in anticipation, hoping to make it quiet enough for him to hear. The ambulance pulled up to the doors, and nurses ran out to greet them. Dr. Martin dropped onto Nan's chest and began to cry loudly. Veronica covered her mouth to keep the sobs from spilling forth. She touched his shoulder in comfort.

"It's okay, Robert. You tried your best," she soothed.

The back doors opened up, and the emergency team grabbed the stretcher and pulled it to the street and took Nan's body indoors to the emergency room.

He shook his head. "I'm sorry, I didn't...I couldn't..." He raised his head to look at Veronica. His eyes were not filled with grief but with guilt.

Veronica's hand flew to her heart in despair as Dr. Martin's shoulders began to silently shake. "What is it?"

They began to shake even harder. "I heard it." He laughed, tears streaming out of the corner of his eyes. "I didn't believe it at first, but I heard her heartbeat! Veronica, Nan's alive!"

They both looked in wonder at the hospital stretcher being rolled into the first emergency room, as doctor after doctor ran in to take care of a living, breathing Nan. The paramedics from the front seat turned to look at the motley crew in the back seat and started cheering.

CHAPTER 19

While it wasn't the full recovery that Mina had hoped for, it was better than being dead. Nan's heart started beating and she was breathing on her own, but she was in a deep coma. It didn't matter to Veronica; all that mattered was that her baby was alive.

What confused Mina was the fact that she was still in a coma. That wasn't part of the bargain, but she did try to recall her words with Maeve. Well, she had fought for Nan, but obviously it wasn't enough. She changed — she was more angry than confused. It wasn't until she cornered Ever at school that she got some answers.

"What is going on, pixie!" Mina hissed into the Fae's ear before first period. The slamming of locker doors helped disguise Mina's words. "I had a talk with Maeve. Apparently she isn't keeping her end of the deal."

Ever turned on Mina with eyes blazing angrily. "How dare you talk about the Fates that way?"

"Fates? What's with the plural anyway? Are you telling me Maeve is one of the ruling Fae?" Mina asked, bewildered.

"How dumb are you? Of course she is. She's our Queen. Haven't you ever heard of the royal 'we' when speaking? When we speak of our royals, it's always 'Fates.'" Ever pulled out her books and shut her locker door. She walked quickly, trying to outpace Mina.

Mina wasn't letting her get away. "Yeah, whatever. I'm talking about this bargain I made with Maeve, and she didn't keep her end." She picked up her speed to keep Ever from outdistancing her.

"You don't get to call her by her first name. To you, Grimm, it's either 'Fates' or 'Queen.' But did you ever stop to ask yourself if you'd kept your end of the bargain? The Fates aren't dumb." Ever turned into her classroom and blocked the door so Mina couldn't enter.

"Don't think you're getting away from me that easily, pixie," Mina hissed out loudly. "I know that your kind is disappearing. Do you want it getting out that you're here in this school? Do you want to disappear like Mrs. Porter?" She was done with playing the helpless heroine; she had best friends to save and a family to protect.

Ever paled at Mina's empty threat. "Meet me after school at the football field."

The second bell rang, signaling the start of class and Mina's obvious tardiness. She didn't care. Mina stared at Ever as the door closed and the pixie went and took her seat in class. Mina slipped down the hallway silently and entered her homeroom class. Mrs. Colbert was subbing and gave Mina a very pointed look as she humbly took her seat.

It was hard to listen to announcements when they came from someone other than the grey-haired teacher. Mrs. Porter's absence was a reminder of Mina's failings and her current bargain. New rumors began to creep up about their missing teacher and how it wasn't an early retirement, but a possible kidnapping. No one knew what was going on, and only Mina knew that she wasn't coming back.

Brody didn't come to school, and actually in most of Mina's classes the attendance was low. There was a vigil going on at the hospital, and under any other circumstance, Mina would've been there. But she knew deep down that her presence at a vigil wasn't going to help Nan.

Once the last bell rang, Mina left her books in her locker and sprinted outside and toward the football field. She knew there was a good possibility that Ever would evade her and run away. She knew that the pixie hated her. When Ever actually showed up, Mina was surprised.

"Yeah, yeah, don't get your panties in a bunch. I'm here," Ever snarled at Mina, brushing past her to sit on the cold steel bleachers. "So I'm sure you've got tons of questions — ask away." She did a little flourish with her hand to add to her sarcasm.

"Maeve promised me that she could save my friend Nan. And if she did, then I would find the Fae who stole the Grimoire. Well, she lied. She didn't save Nan. Nan is in a coma in the hospital!" Mina was pacing back and forth in front of the bored Ever.

"Hold it, hold it." Ever held up her hands, and Mina stopped to look at her. "What were the Fates' actual words?"

Mina's face scrunched up in thought and repeated her conversation to Ever.

Ever held up her fingertips to her temples and closed her eyes as if contemplating. "Anything else, O mortal one?"

"Oh, and she said 'I cannot save her fully, but I can give you a fighting chance to save her,'" Mina rushed out.

Ever opened one eye in disbelief at Mina. "That's it?"

Mina looked at Ever hopefully. "Yeah, that was it. So can you tell me what happened?"

Ever jumped down off of the bleacher and started walking away. "Yeah, stupid, you didn't finish your end of the bargain. Get back the Grimoire and finish your quest. By the way, that will be fourteen ninety five — I take cash or check."

Mina shook her head confused. "But Maeve said I failed my quest. So what is there to finish? I thought she would bring my friend back." Mina began following Ever down the stairs to the field.

"Do I have to spell it out for you? We have rules. We like to bend those rules, um, usually to benefit us. But her Highness didn't bring your friend back to life because she wouldn't. It's because she couldn't. We aren't all-powerful, as some people think we are. But we are pretty good at manipulating things."

Mina stopped walking and stood there, dumbfounded, waiting for an answer.

Ever turned back and walked up to Mina and began tapping her on the head. "Hello, Mina! She revamped your quest. Instead of your buddy being dead, she put her to sleep, like the old sleeping princess tales, Snow White and Sleeping Beauty. You get another chance to finish this tale the right way. I'm sure once you complete it, your friend will wake up good as new. Just so long as you find the Grimoire and stop whoever is trying to kidnap us."

A light went on in Mina's head. She had just assumed that she had failed the quest and that was it. She wouldn't get a second chance to save Nan. But that didn't help her in trying to find out who had taken the Grimoire.

"So how do I find the person who stole the Grimoire? I don't even know how to tell if someone is Fae or not. I mean, it could be anybody."

"Gimp!" Ever dropped her backpack and began to fumble with a keychain that was attached to a zipper. "Here, it's not that powerful, and you don't want to go flashing it around at just anybody. You can really tick off the wrong kind of Fae and get in a lot of trouble. But this will help." She tossed Mina a small blue cylinder attached to a keychain.

She looked at it in disbelief. "A laser pointer? How in the world is that supposed to help?" She clicked it on and flashed it at Ever, and nothing happened until Mina waved it over Ever's back; the air began to waver, and her purple and blue wings appeared. "Hey, I can see your wings."

"Yeah, we try to blend in as much as we can, but sometimes a strong laser can cut through both planes and ruin our disguises. It won't work on any of the Royals, though."

"Royals, are they like the Fates?" Mina asked timidly.

"They are those who are blood relation to the Fates. Because of that, they are shifters and are powerful enough to withstand a laser pointer." She snorted in laughter.

Mina nodded her head, thinking. "Hey, Ever," Mina said quietly, trying not to offend the girl. "Do you think Jared's disappearance is linked to the person who is imprisoning your kind in the Grimoire?"

Ever snorted and rolled her eyes. "You don't even know the half of what's going on. But I can tell you that wherever the Grimoire is, Jared is sure to be close by."

"You don't think he's the one behind the kidnappings..."

"NO! He is not." Ever became angry and turned on Mina. "If you knew him, you would know that isn't possible."

Mina felt her anger rise to match Ever's. "Hey, I know it could be possible. He did kidnap me and abandon me in the woods. I'm just asking because I have to." They had walked out of the football field and were next to the bike rack. Mina pulled out her red Schwinn and put up the kickstand. She paused to look at Ever, trying to see beyond her tough exterior. Beneath the heavy eye makeup, gelled hair, and black and purple clothes, she saw a young and scared girl.

"Why are you still here? I mean, why don't you just go back to the Fae world where it's safer?" Mina asked.

Ever's head dropped to her chest and her dark bangs fell over her eyes, hiding her face. "Who said anything about the Fae world being safer? We all have things we're running from.

Besides, who says a girl can't attend school? Even a human school, for that matter. It's not like there is a law forbidding it," she snapped back testily.

Mina tried to apologize. "I didn't mean anything…"

"Sure you did. You think we don't belong here, that we should go home to the Fae world. Well, let me tell you something, Mina Grime. I *am* home. This is my home. So excuse me if I'm not super excited about helping you finish your quests so we are forced to go back to the Fae world. Not all of us want to go back. Sure, we may have jobs that require us to go back, but a lot of us prefer to live here."

"I'm sorry, I didn't think," Mina started.

"You never think. No — no one does." Ever shrugged her shoulders and stuffed her hands into her jacket. She waved off Mina before putting in her ear buds, making a big deal about turning on her iPod and walking away.

CHAPTER 20

It was a long shot, but the only one Mina could think of in her current circumstances. She had waited, somewhat impatiently, until her overly protective mother and her younger brother had gone to sleep before slipping into the bathroom and stealing the mirror. It wasn't stealing exactly; she planned on putting their bathroom mirror back, as long as she didn't break it like she did the other one. It was big, but thankfully it had a thick metal frame around it, which made it easier to carry up the fire escape to her retreat.

She had decided to try her idea on the roof instead of talking to the mirror in the bathroom and freaking out her mother and brother. Yeah, it was better on the roof. If she didn't break her neck trying to maneuver it up there.

Finally, Mina got the mirror safely to the rooftop and placed it on the ledge next to her salvaged gnome statue, Sir Nomer. She took a few steps back and frowned thoughtfully at her own reflection, biting the inside of her cheek in thought. What should she do? Normally Jared just appeared to her out of the blue at the most inconvenient times, but now she needed him right now.

Jared was the only clue she had to finding out who had the Grimoire. If he was trapped like the others, then maybe he could give her a clue as to his whereabouts or who had kidnapped him. That was, if he ever decided to show his face.

"Hello?" Mina called warily to the mirror. She waved her hand in front of it awkwardly. "Psst, Jared. Hey, I'm here now. You can come out whenever you want. I need your help!"

Nothing. The mirror only reflected her image back at her.

"I knew this would happen. I shouldn't have expected anything different from the likes of you!" She turned her back on the mirror and mimed storming away, peeking over her shoulder to see if there was any change in the mirror. Nada.

"This is ridiculous!" Mina hissed out loud. She came back to the mirror and touched the frame, and thought long and hard about what she wanted. It wasn't like she had any power over the mirror or anything, and or could turn it on whenever she wanted like a TV...or did she?

Her own mother's words came back to haunt her, and she could hear Sara, clear as day, saying, "You don't always get to choose the part you play in the quests."

That was it; she had thought she was going to be the protector or the hunter who saved the princess from the evil queen. But it was her own bitter jealousy that had turned the tale on her. Mina was the villain! It was the Story using her own emotions against her and trying to harm her best friend. It was probably all set up to entrap Savannah White, who by all means would make the perfect princess, but at the time, it had been Nan whom she was the most jealous of.

If that was true, then Mina did have power over the mirror. There was only one true way to test it to see if she was the jealous queen in the Snow White tale. Mina slowly walked back to the mirror and stared at her own pale reflection. Her voice quivered with nervousness as she tried to remember what the words were.

"M-m-mirror, mirror, on the wall, who's the f-fairest of them all?" She closed her eyes tightly and felt her heartbeat speed up. A small hum began to emanate from the mirror, and a swirling vortex appeared. She dropped her head in shame, and tears of regret poured from her eyes, but she knew she had to open her eyes to see what the mirror was going to show her.

It came as no surprise when a hospital room appeared in the mirror, although the view was skewed, as if the mirror could only reflect to her from another reflective surface in the room. It took a minute for Mina to recognize the angle she was viewing from. It was the dark TV screen. She knew the room, had been there the first night, and recognized the sleeping blonde form in the hospital bed. It was Nan.

So the tale was playing out truthfully: Nan was the fairest, and Mina was the jealous queen. She was about to close the view from the mirror when the hospital door opened and a young, handsome blond-haired boy walked into view. He kept his back to the TV screen and went to sit by the bed, facing Nan and hiding his identity.

He spoke softly, and Mina was surprised when she actually heard his voice through the mirror. Apparently, the sound worked if the mirror was used right. The young man reached out and grasped Nan's hand, holding it in his own. He whispered the same two words over and over, and finally they reached Mina's ears.

Mina's back stiffened in surprise, hurt, and anger. She recognized that voice; she knew the shape of those shoulders. It was Brody. Brody was sitting beside Nan's bed, comforting her and talking to her, when it should be her job.

She backed up in anger and waved the image away, surprised when it actually disappeared on command — but, then again, she wasn't. She paced the small rooftop, clenching her fists and trying not to cry. She had to distance herself from the situation; she couldn't worry about Nan right now. She knew she was safe, at least for now. Confirming the mirror theory and proving the quest she was in gave Mina the answer of how to save Nan. But it didn't help her with the task of finding the Grimoire or contacting Jared.

"Okay, think, Mina. Think!" she commanded herself, while trying to calm her nerves and emotions. Quickly, she wiped the tears away and went to stand before the mirror again.

"Mirror, mirror, on the wall, show me the one I hate most of all."

The mirror swirled again, and Mina gagged and jumped back in disgust as an overly large mouth appeared in front of the mirror. The mouth smiled, puckered, and a giant tube of lipstick appeared and gave another coating of frost pink to the lips.

"Gah!" Mina cried out when the view finally pulled back and she could see that those lips belonged to none other than Savannah White. The image was coming from her makeup compact. "Okay, let's try that again." She waved the image away.

"How do I rhyme it to get Jared to appear?" It wasn't until she sat in the chair and stared at her Sir Nomer statue that she got the final idea. "Thanks to you, Sir Nomer, I think I have it." She stood up and walked before the mirror, her shoulders straight, and her chin up in forced confidence.

In a loud and commanding voice she spoke once again to the mirror. "Mirror, mirror, on the wall, show me the one who thinks Sir Nomer is a dumb name for a doll."

She held her breath and waited. The mirror swirled again, and this time another face came into focus, one that was definitely not happy.

"It is about time you figured it out, Mina!" Jared grumbled through the mirror.

CHAPTER 21

His arms were crossed in annoyance, and his dark grey eyes were stormy. "I can't believe it took you so long to figure it out. The audio doesn't exactly work if I try to summon you from my end, if you may recall. But what can you expect when I try to mimic a Disney movie?"

Mina didn't realize how much she had missed Jared until she saw him before her in the mirror. Despite the annoyed look on his face and his clenched jaw, she was genuinely happy to see him. "Jared, it worked!"

"Of course, it worked. I've been trying to give you hints long enough. I can't believe it took you this long to speak to a mirror. I thought all girls talked to a mirror. Sheesh!" Even though he played at being angry, she could see the slight twitch in his mouth as he tried to hold back his happiness at seeing her.

"Jared, where are you? Is the Grimoire with you? Are you safe? Are there others with you?" She spoke quickly, nervously, and felt as if she rambled at a mile a minute.

He held up his hands and looked around his surroundings carefully. He seemed tired and worn out, but physically unharmed. "I'm all right. Yes, the Grimoire is with me, and no, there are no others with me. They are all imprisoned within the book, but I think we can free them."

"Where are you, Jared? Who's got you?" Mina whispered in kind, feeling his urgency and the need for quiet.

"Mina, I'm at the hospital. We're leaving, but he's coming back tomorrow night."

"Who's coming back? Who's got you, Jared? What do you mean, you're leaving?"

He sighed and ran his hands through his hair in frustration. "I can't explain everything right now, Mina. It would take too long. You have to trust me on this."

"Ha, like I'm ever going to trust you again!" She pointed her finger and jabbed it at the mirror as if trying to poke him.

"Mina, I never left you," he said softly. "I've never once left your side, unless you left me."

"But why aren't you imprisoned within the book as well? Oh, wait. You — you said the book doesn't work on you. Why doesn't the book work on you, Jared?"

Jared ignored her. "Mina, it's going to kill Nan."

"What? Who would do something that awful? Jared, you should call the police." Mina began to panic and felt her voice rise in nervousness.

Jared raised his eyebrows to remind her of the obvious reason. "I can't call the police, Mina."

"Well, then, tell me who's going to kill Nan. I'll call the police."

"And tell them what exactly? It's a Reaper, Mina." he said sadly.

"Reaper? Jared, I don't know what that is," she spat out in frustration.

Jared leaned close to the mirror, his eyes filled with sadness. "Yes, you do. You've heard of the Grimm Reaper before, but you never made the connection to your family. The Grimms don't usually die from failing the quests, Mina. They die from meeting a Grimm Reaper. They are hunters who track and hunt the Grimms for sport. This one in particular — I recognized its scent. It was the one who killed your father."

Mina felt like screaming in anger. Her blood boiled, and she clenched her jaw.

"When, Jared? When is it planning on killing her?" her voice trembled.

She saw Jared swallow in nervousness. "Mina, don't come. It's a trap. Don't do it."

"I'm not asking again, Jared," she demanded.

"Tomorrow night. Midnight. The reaping hour."

CHAPTER 22

This was absolutely the worst possible idea ever in the history of history. She paced the front porch of the Carmichaels' three-story mansion while biting her thumb. She had already lied to security about why she was here. It was easy, considering she had used the same excuse the first time she came to the Carmichaels to drop off a pamphlet of information from Happy Maids, the company her mom worked for. Well, since that got her in the first time, she didn't see any reason for it not to get her in the second time. And it worked.

Now she was a pile of nerves and had no real reason for being here. Except that she really, really needed to talk to Brody. Nobody answered when she rang the doorbell, and she was beginning to think that they were purposely avoiding her. One of the gardeners who was tending the bushes waved at her to get her attention and pointed to the back of the house.

Mina knew what was back there; she had seen it when she walked up the driveway. It was the stables. Even though they were in the suburbs, the Carmichaels owned enough property to raise horses. Races, jumps, or show; you name it, the Carmichaels competed in it. She followed the stone walkway around the side of the mansion and down the pathway past the large Olympic-size outdoor pool, which was currently set up with a net in the middle of it, probably so Brody could practice water polo. Luckily, no one was swimming, which left one other place to look. Mina shuddered. The stables.

Of course, he couldn't be good at just one thing; he had to be great at everything. She could see him in the distance on a beautiful thoroughbred, taking her through the course. He was extremely soft-spoken when giving commands, and Mina could see that he had an easy way with the horse. When they were both ready, they lined up. One second they were still, and the next they flew over, around, and back. He was handsome in black pants, riding boots, and a helmet. He looked dashing and debonair. Mina looked down at her jeans, button-down blue coat, and flats, and felt out of place. She pulled on her messy braid and tried to straighten it, without success.

Every time the horse jumped, Mina held her breath in terror, scared that he would fall off and be trampled. The horse didn't miss a jump or a stride; only on the second-to-last jump did she knock a pole down. Mina made it to the fence and waited to be noticed before speaking, unsure of what her reception would be, since the last time they had spoken she had blamed him for Nan's death.

The horse noticed her first and turned to look at her. Brody looked up in surprise, and then he frowned. Yeah, Mina had known it was a bad idea to come. Before either one of them could say anything, she turned and began to walk back up the hill toward the house.

Seconds later, she could hear hoof beats close behind her. Mina looked up when Brody rode up next to her. She decided to speak first.

"So it's pretty obvious that you're not sick or injured," Mina accused him.

"No, I'm fine," he answered, slowing the horse and sliding off to walk next to Mina. His eyes were hollow, and it looked like he hadn't slept in days.

"So why didn't you go to school?" she asked.

"Because I couldn't face you," he said simply. He hung his head in shame, and Mina wanted to reach out and touch the soft blond hair. She held herself in check. "You blame me for what happened. She's your best friend, and I killed her."

Tears started to burn at the corner of Mina's eyes, but her anger and jealousy of Brody and Nan in a car together held them back. "What were you two doing that night?" Mina asked angrily.

Brody paused, caught off guard by her angry tone. He looked guilty, and he turned to look at his horse. "Peter's band had to leave shortly after the rain started and everyone went inside. They had a gig in the next state, so they had to be at the airport in a few hours. There was some sort of tiff between them, and he left without saying goodbye to her."

"That's hard to believe. They looked pretty happy together most of the night — I can't imagine what it could possibly have been about," Mina grumbled, crossing her arms in a defensive stance.

"It was over you." Brody shrugged.

"What?" Mina felt a knot form in her stomach, a hard ball of jealousy that was quickly unraveling.

"I don't know all the details — something about wanting to find you but his needing to leave. So, anyway, they didn't say goodbye, and he was going to be gone for a month. She begged me to drive her to the airport so she could say goodbye." He looked at Mina and quickly glanced away.

"But why you? Why didn't she drive herself or get someone else to take her?" Mina demanded, her face betraying her jealousy.

"Because I was one of the last cars in and the easiest to get out. She didn't want her mom to know. She thought we could catch them in time and get back before anyone found out. It was stupid, I know. And now you must hate me for killing her." He cleared his throat and refused to look at her. It was obvious he wasn't handling this very well.

"Um, earth to Brody. She's in a coma, not dead." Mina stopped and grabbed his arm and held on tightly.

He tried to shake her off. "I can't, Mina! You weren't there — you weren't in the car. You didn't see her, I did! She was dead." He was so angry his horse started to get finicky.

She knew she needed to calm him down. She took a deep breath and spoke slowly, clearly, so he could hear her heartfelt plea. "I'm sorry for the way I spoke to you. I was angry. But you have got to believe me when I say you have got to get over it. Nan's not dead — she's alive! You can't beat yourself up over the past."

He shrugged angrily and looked off into the distance, purposely avoiding answering Mina.

Mina spoke with conviction, and the words almost caught in her throat, but she forced them out. "I don't blame you, Brody, for anything. It's not your fault, Brody. If anyone's to blame, it's me."

Brody turned and looked at her sharply, surprise evident in his blue eyes, but behind that she saw the pain and the guilt. Mina felt herself go weak, and she reached out to touch his cheek. He leaned into her palm and breathed in the scent of her hand. Mina's breath caught in her throat at the intimate feel of his skin and the way he pushed against her.

Slowly, he dropped his horse's reins and moved closer to her; Mina anticipated the hug and leaned up as he wrapped his arms around her. He buried his face in her neck and hugged her. She closed her eyes and let herself enjoy the comfort of his arms, until she felt him shaking softly. He was crying. Mina was saddened, but only slightly. What she wanted more than ever was his love; what he needed right now was comfort. She found herself rubbing his back and telling him that she was going to fix everything. She promised.

When he pulled away, Mina wanted to pull him closer and kiss him. But she knew it wasn't the time to confess her feelings.

She sighed loudly and finally decided to tell him why she came. "I need your help. I know this sounds stupid, but I think I know a way to wake up Nan from the coma. But first I need a ride someplace. Then I will tell you my somewhat brilliant plan, but it involves calling your very famous cousin and convincing him to make an unplanned tour stop."

CHAPTER 23

It was seven o'clock when they first pulled up to the hospital parking garage. They both signed in at the visitor center and got their red and white visitor tags. Mina stopped in the gift shop and bought the cheapest stuffed rabbit she could find and carried it up to Nan's room.

Visiting mostly consisted of sitting quietly next to Nan and staring at the door, waiting for nurses and doctors to make their rounds. It was boring, but Brody didn't mind at all. He was the one who kept speaking to Nan and acting all concerned when the first nurse came in to check her vitals.

Mina never told Brody her full plan; she just told him enough to make it believable. She said she knew that Nan was going to wake up if Peter and Brody were both there to apologize. She knew it wouldn't work, but she wanted to be there when anybody walked into her best friend's hospital room.

When the first nurse came in, Brody stood up and let her approach Nan. Mina sat in a corner chair and pulled out her laser pointer keychain. When the nurse turned her back, Mina ran that laser pointer all over the nurse head to toe, waiting for a waver or a change of any kind. Nothing. This nurse wasn't Fae.

After she left, Mina waited twenty minutes, then asked Brody to push the call button. A different nurse came in and asked what the problem was. Brody lied beautifully and said he thought Nan was waking up.

Mina scanned this nurse with the laser pointer as well and was actually caught by the nurse, who only gave her a disapproving stare. When she left, Mina felt helpless. "This is never going to work. I have to get more nurses and doctors in here at one time."

"Why?" Brody asked.

"Because I think one of them is a fraud, and I don't believe they are here to help Nan," Mina said, without really believing Brody would understand.

"You think it would really help Nan?" he asked.

"I know it would if I could just see all of the people who are assigned to Nan. I know I can find the fraud." She slumped back in her chair.

"And you can tell this just by looking at them?" he asked. She nodded. He took a moment and thought about it long and hard before standing up and walking over to Nan's heart monitor. He looked at Mina and smiled. "Are you ready for Armageddon?" He reached for her chest.

"Brody! What are you doing?" Mina gasped.

"I saw this in a movie once. You may want to stand back. I'm about to get in serious trouble." He winked at Mina and reached for the heart monitor wire that was stuck to Nan's chest. With a quick tug, the adhesive released, and the beeping stopped. The monitor flatlined, and an alarm went off.

Brody jumped away from Nan but wasn't quick enough as nurses ran into the room, followed by Dr. Martin.

"Now, look carefully," Brody whispered loudly as he backed away from the bed.

Mina used the distraction to wave the laser pointer over everyone who entered the room — even Dr. Martin, who was on duty — when they rushed inside, but nothing. They were all human. When one of the nurses found the detached wire, she attached it and gave both of them a loud and angry warning.

Dr. Martin turned to Mina and Brody and was surprised by their presence. "What are you two doing here?"

"We are worried for Nan. I think someone is trying to hurt her," Mina rushed out.

Dr. Martin looked disgusted by Mina's outburst. "I told you that if you did anything that would influence or harm my future daughter-in-law that there would be serious consequences."

"But, Dr. Martin," Brody cut in. "We didn't harm her."

Dr. Martin exploded. He took his clipboard and threw it on a chair. "How dare you stand here and tell me that you didn't harm Nan?" He pointed his finger angrily at Brody. "You crashed a car with her in it. And you!" He turned to Mina. "I don't care what anyone else says, you are no longer allowed to see, speak, or talk to Nan. Do you hear me?"

Nurse Diedre walked in and looked at the commotion her boss was causing. Dr. Martin motioned to the large nurse. "See that these two leave the building. They are never to enter this room." He plopped himself down into a chair next to Nan's bed and rested his face in his hands.

Brody and Mina were forced out, and their guard, the surly Nurse Diedre, took absolute pleasure in walking them down the hallways and out the front doors. She said very little, but when they both stepped onto the sidewalk, she spoke one sentence. "Stupid Gimp, always causing trouble." She turned with a victorious smile and walked back into the hospital.

Mina gasped out loud, pulled the laser out of her pocket, and flashed it across Nurse Diedre. At first nothing happened. Then her white uniform began to waver, and for a split second Mina could see something underneath the uniform — SCALES. Nurse Diedre was the Reaper.

"It's her," Mina cried out, grabbing onto Brody's shirt. "She's the one that's going to hurt Nan!"

Brody reached out and pulled Mina toward him in an embrace. "Not if we can help it."

~~~

Three hours later, a very large and expensive tour bus pulled up to the hospital parking lot. Mina and Brody jumped up from the curb and ran to greet the Dead Prince Society tour bus. The doors opened, and music blasted from the speakers. Naga, wearing skinny jeans and a black vest, strode down the steps and opened his arms wide, addressing his sparse audience.

"Did someone call for a tall glass of hotness?" Naga howled, motioning to himself and jumped down to the sidewalk. He strutted around, looking for fans, and his shoulders dropped when he didn't see any. He reached up to tenderly touch his white striped mohawk.

"Relax, you look beautiful, darlin'," Constantine teased Naga as he swung out of the bus. "I'm sure you will knock the nurses dead." Naga turned to take a swing at the longhaired band member, who ducked at the last minute. Magnus stepped out and immediately asked if the cafeteria was open, followed by Peter, who appeared half dead.

His hair looked as if it hadn't been washed in days, and his clothes looked like he had slept in them. Brody walked over to him and asked if they could speak in private. Brody spoke quietly, and Peter nodded his head and ran his fingers through his hair.

Brody's shoulders slumped, and Mina could only guess that he was admitting to Peter that he was the one driving the car that led to the accident. Peter's body stiffened in anger, and he turned and punched Brody in the face. Brody wasn't expecting it and was knocked to the pavement.

Peter stood above Brody, yelling down at him. "I blame you for this, and I'll talk to you about this later. But right now I want to know how we can help Nan." He turned to face a stunned Mina and his band mates.

"Are you up for making a little bit of noise?" Mina asked hopefully.

"At this time of night, we will probably draw in complaints and bring the cops." Magnus had found a bag of chips and was crunching them loudly. A moment later a van pulled up behind the bus, and their stagehands got out to see what was going on.

Naga shrugged. "I ain't afraid of no coppers. It will get us on TV, no doubt."

Constantine went to the storage compartments under the tour bus and unlocked the first unit, pulling out a large speaker and guitar. "Let's do it," he answered. Constantine handed one of the waiting stage crew a box of microphone cords. "I'm ready for an impromptu concert. What about you, Pete?"

Peter ignored Constantine and walked over to Mina. "Are you sure that this is going to help?" he asked, his eyes filled with hope and pain.

She shook her head. "Not really, but this is only the first part of my plan. The second will come later. Are you in? Right now I need you to be as loud as you can. I need all of the attention on you guys so I can sneak in. Will you do this for Nan?" Mina pleaded.

Magnus began to set up his drums. Naga was pulling out extension cords, and Constantine walked over with a large black guitar case. Peter unzipped the case and pulled out the very large red guitar he had used at his last concert. Chills raced up Mina's arms as Peter pulled the strap over his head. He took a cord from a stagehand and plugged it into his guitar.

More stage crew appeared and began to set up the portable sound system and lights. Brody jumped right in and began to help organize the equipment.

Quickly the band began to tune their instruments. Cords and wires were run from the buses to various transformer boxes in the bushes of the hospital. A few hospital security guards came to see what was going on, but so far none of them had approached the band. Mina looked up and saw the curtain in Nan's room move slightly. Someone was in there already. She hoped it wasn't the Reaper.

"Please, hurry!" Mina pleaded; sweat broke out on her forehead as she checked her watch again. It was 11:45 p.m. Fifteen minutes to midnight.

Brody ran a microphone and a stand out, and placed it in front of Peter. They both glared at each other angrily.

"We don't have time," Mina pointed out.

Peter closed his eyes for a moment and took a deep shuddering breath. He opened them and pasted on a wide fake smile, transforming instantly into Valdemar, the lead singer. "One concert to wake the dead coming up." He opened up his mouth and began to sing.

~~~

It was working. People began to rush to the windows and hallways, and even down to the first floor to see what all of the commotion was. Mina was surprised to see how many of the hospital staff were excited by the concert. To them it was an unexpected treat. And because the band was in the parking lot, they didn't really try to stop it. But eventually someone would. Someone would call the cops, and then the hospital would be swarming with police. The more police there were, the more likely the Reaper would give up and run away. Who was going to try to kill a girl if the hospital was surrounded by police? No one. Or at least Mina hoped that no one would. But then, if the Reaper was a nurse, she could slip Nan any kind of drugs and no one would be the wiser.

She used the Dead Prince Society as a distraction and rushed through the emergency entrance doors. Since most of the hospital staff had gone to take pictures at the front of the hospital, she found it a fairly easy route to take. She bypassed the elevator and took the stairs two at a time to Nan's floor. Mina opened the stairwell door and listened for sounds of hospital staff. There were none. She slipped onto the floor and tiptoed down the hall, pausing when she had to cross the waiting room.

As she expected, most of the night staff was at the window, looking out onto the scene below. She could hear them whispering furiously, deciding how they were going to take turns and go down to get autographs. Nurse Diedre and Dr. Martin were nowhere to be seen among the window gawkers.

Mina was just going to have to take a chance that they weren't about. As she moved silently toward Nan's room, Mina began to doubt herself and her plan. Maybe she should have just called the police and told them someone was going to try to kill her best friend. But then, what if they didn't believe her? She shook her head in frustration. She would have been taken in for questioning and asked how she knew all of this. What was she going to tell them? That a boy in a mirror told her a Grimm Reaper was going to kill Nan at midnight? It wasn't happening.

"I knew you would try and sneak back in," a gravelly voice said close to Mina's ear. "You shouldn't be here."

She turned to see that Nurse Diedre had come up behind her. Her grey hair was still pulled into a tight knot. Her plump arms reached out to grab her, but Mina ran forward. She ran down the hall away from Nan's room, hoping to lead the Fae away. The nurse was right on her tail. Mina turned down a flight of stairs and through another hallway, ignoring yellow signs and construction tape. She ducked through a set of double doors and ran through two sheets of plastic and froze. The smell of sheetrock, dust, and paint assailed her nose. She had unintentionally run into an unfinished wing of the hospital.

It was a long wing, with tall metal beams, half-finished walls, and supplies stacked randomly around the room. Looking around for cover, she saw a large pallet of sheetrock. Mina ducked behind it and tried to make her breathing softer. A few seconds later, she heard the same double doors open with a creak, followed by the swishing sound of plastic slowly being moved to the side.

She could hear Diedre looking for her, her feet slowly moving across the cement floor. But then something changed; the sound became louder, and the floor vibrated with each step. She could hear breathing, and it was loud. Mina peeked around the corner of her hiding place and could see billows of dust floating up on the other side of the room where Diedre was. No, wait. It wasn't dust; it was smoke.

Mina heard a gurgling sound, as if something was snuffing and breathing loudly. She froze in extreme terror, her mind trying to put together what she'd seen with the laser pointer with what she was hearing. It wasn't good. A metal clang rang out, and Mina looked across the room toward where the sound originated. She could barely see the crowbar that had fallen to the floor. Her heart raced and thudded loudly in her chest.

She didn't need to see what was hunting her to know that Diedre had transformed into her Fae form, and she was coming closer to Mina's hiding spot. Mina crawled on her hands and knees and moved over to a large pile of wood beams seconds before Diedre came around the corner.

From her new hiding spot, she could see the Fae, and it terrified Mina. She was a dragon. Not the pretty fairy tale kind, but more of a shorter, stockier version. It walked and slithered on four legs and moved very much like a lizard. It was silver and black, and it coughed puffs of smoke. The dragon leaned down and sniffed the area that Mina had moments ago vacated.

She was doomed; there was no way Mina could kill the dragon, especially when she didn't have the Grimoire. At most, she could maybe harm it or distract it while she got Nan out of the hospital. But she was running out of time and out of hiding places. The dragon was beginning to pick up speed in its search. As if it was the one becoming more desperate.

Her hands were clammy with nervousness, and it finally dawned on Mina what she had going for her. As she watched the dragon maneuver through the large room, she found its weakness. The dragon wasn't very fast. The ceilings were too low for it to use its wings, and so it was forced to amble around on its four legs. If she ran, she could outrun it.

She ducked to the ground and began to crawl across the room to the spot where she had seen the crowbar fall. Mina's hand reached out to grab it, and she saw the tool belt next to it, left by a construction worker. Grabbing a hammer, Mina counted to three and tossed it as far as she could in the corner away from the double doors. It clanged loudly, and she heard the dragon roar in excitement and rush to the corner.

Mina was finding it very hard to breathe, as the room was becoming dense with smoke. But she took a deep breath, and as soon as the dragon passed her, she took off running toward the double doors.

The dragon turned its deep blue, angry eyes on Mina and changed directions to chase after her. Mina screamed in fright when she reached the doors and pushed them closed as soon as she exited. Turning, she could see the dragon bearing down upon her through the glass slits. Clenching her teeth, she thrust the crowbar through the metal handles of the doors just as the dragon tried to bust through. Mina fell onto her backside in fear and watched as the large metal doors held firm. Smoke billowed out beneath the door every time the Fae pushed against the crowbar, but they didn't budge. A large blue eye appeared in the doors window and looked at her angrily.

She swallowed her fear, dusted herself off, and ran back upstairs toward Nan, praying that the doors would hold until Nan was safe. Once she was back on the fourth floor, she walked quickly down the hallway, noticing the red and blue lights flashing on the wall when she passed a window. Someone had finally called the police. And now with police on the premises, all she had to do was get Nan out of the hospital and somewhere safe. She could try to track down the Reaper again and get the Grimoire back on a different day. She knew the Reaper wouldn't give up; she would eventually try to kill Mina. But by then, Mina would have found a way to kill a dragon.

Mina came to room 413 and quietly opened the door, slipping inside. The room was dark and the drapes closed, with just a flicker of red and blue lights dancing on the ceiling. She couldn't hear any music, which meant the impromptu concert was officially over. Walking over to the bed, Mina stumbled over something on the floor. She reached around in the near darkness to move the object, and her hand came in contact with a warm leg, and it was attached to a body. Mina pulled her hand away quickly and looked up to see that Nan was still asleep and her heart monitor was still quietly beeping.

Slowly, she moved around the bed and reached for the light switch next to the hospital bed. Her hand shook with fear. Quickly, like pulling off a Band-Aid, she flicked on the light and looked at the body on the floor. It was Dr. Martin. There was a large lump on the side of his head and blood on his forehead.

Mina reached down to touch Dr. Martin's neck to feel for a pulse, and he moaned softly. He was still alive! A soft beeping sound came from across the room, and Mina looked to the corner to see a man sitting silently in a chair, watching her.

He was dressed from head to toe in black with a long leather jacket that reached the floor. The man reached over and touched the alarm on his expensive watch, shutting it off. She looked at the clock in the room and back to the man in the chair. It was midnight. He slowly stood up and walked toward her, his hand reaching for a long wooden object leaning against the wall.

She shook her head in confusion, not understanding and not believing who she saw. She recognized him. It didn't make sense.

He clicked a button on the side of the wooden staff, and a sword shot out. "You're just in time," Karl said gruffly. "For the reaping!" He swung the sword at Mina's head.

CHAPTER 24

Mina fell backward, tripping once again over Dr. Martin's prone form. Karl smiled cruelly and easily pushed the hospital bed with Nan on it out of the way, exposing a direct path to Mina. What could she do? He could kill any of them at any moment. She could only do one thing. Stall.

"Why now? Why didn't you kill me earlier when you had the chance? I mean, come on now, you had me and let me go. That doesn't sound like you are a very good Reaper," Mina taunted, forcing herself to sound braver than she was.

Karl stopped and bared his teeth angrily, and then he did something unexpected. He laughed, a deep menacing chuckle that only got louder and louder.

He stopped laughing and smiled at her. "It has been quite a few years since I killed my last Grimm, and truthfully, I wasn't expecting to almost run one over."

He moved to the left, and Mina mirrored his movements by moving to the right, keeping out of reach of the sword.

"Well, obviously, we're not all dead," she taunted again, eyeing the blade.

"I had caught wind of a new one arising and was hunting the Grimm." Karl eyed her up and down carefully. "I wasn't expecting one so young. For you to actually lie and tell me you were this girl," he nodded toward Nan, sleeping in the bed, "was brilliant.

"If I had known who you were, I would have instantly killed you in the woods instead of delaying my kill." He reached into his jacket and pulled out a black leather-bound book. Mina stiffened when she saw it. It was the Grimoire, although it looked different since it had changed shape to accommodate its new master.

"That's mine," Mina demanded.

"Was yours." Karl waved the book around. "It's probably the only thing that saved you that night. I hadn't planned on finding this. I didn't recognize what I had, and when I finally figured out it was the fabled Grimoire and that you had lied about who you were, it was too late. Someone had alerted the rangers to where we were. So I took my prize and let you escape. But I knew that if I baited you, and killed this Nan Taylor, you would come to me." He opened his hand in an inviting way and pointed to Mina. "And I was right: Here you are."

"So you're the one imprisoning the Fae in the book," Mina accused him.

Karl shrugged nonchalantly. "They all had it coming. Actually, all of the Fae have it coming, including you."

"What about Jared? What did you do to him?" Mina yelled.

Karl looked at her, confused. "I didn't capture a Jared. Well, not that I know of." He laughed.

Her mouth pursed in thought. She was out of time. She heard a commotion in the hallway that was coming closer, and so did the Reaper. Karl yelled loudly and raised his sword high in the air as the door burst in and Nurse Diedre rushed in, jumping directly into the path of the sword. She screamed and halfway changed shape midair right as the sword cut down onto her silver-scaled shoulder. It embedded itself deep into bone. Her scream dissolved into a roar of pain as she collapsed to the ground. The sword had broken in two — half stuck in the dragon Diedre, the other half held pathetically in a very nervous Reaper's hand.

The old nurse, beaten and battered, pulled herself up and changed fully into her dragon form, backing the Reaper into the corner. He tried to dive right, but she clawed at his jacket and ripped open the pocket containing the Grimoire.

Mina saw it fall out and skitter across the floor. She dove for it, but so did Karl. Right when he grabbed the Grimoire, Diedre bit down on his leg. He screamed and reached into his jacket for another of his reaping weapons — a wickedly curved blade, which he stabbed into the dragon's nose.

Mina didn't look back; she didn't have time. She fumbled and pulled Dr. Martin up to a standing position, and rolled him onto the foot of Nan's bed. He was barely on. She unplugged Nan from the machines and began to roll the hospital bed toward the open door, giving thanks that the new hospital rooms were large enough to accommodate a moving bed and a large dragon.

She swung the bed into the hallway and looked back toward the door to see a large gust of flame erupt out of the room. She could hear the sound of fighting and smell the smoke of the dragon. Mina needed to get people out of the hospital, and fast. On the wall was a red fire alarm, and she pulled it. Immediately, the alarm went off, and the few night staff who weren't downstairs watching the police commotion outside began to evacuate the hospital rooms. Thankfully, Nan's room was the only one occupied down her hallway. When a nurse began to run toward the room filled with fire, the dragon, and Reaper, Mina intercepted her.

"Hey! Don't go down there — there's a fire. I managed to get them out, but I need you to take them."

The nurse, whose name tag read "Mandy," looked down the hall to where Mina pointed. Her eyes widened in fright and her training kicked in; she grabbed the bed and began to push toward the emergency exit. Mina could see the patients who were strong enough to walk being escorted toward the stairs. Others were lifted and carried.

Looking down the hall, Mina saw the nurse wave to a young man who did a fireman lift on the doctor and head down the stairs. Mandy scooped up Nan and carried her down herself. They were the last to exit the floor. Satisfied that they would be safe, Mina ran back toward the room.

The floor rumbled under her feet, and then a wall crashed outward as Diedre and Karl fell into the hallway. Karl stabbed the dragon again, but Diedre used her large claws to rake down his stomach. Unbelievably, he wasn't sustaining as much damage as the dragon. The dragon bit his arm, and a loud metallic crunch was heard.

Mina grabbed a fire extinguisher from the wall and ran back into the burning room. She used the extinguisher to clear a path to look through the fiery rubble. Somewhere in this wreckage was the Grimoire. Smoke burned her eyes, and she dropped to the ground to stay below the rising smoke.

There it was. The Grimoire was in a pile of debris by the wall. She used the extinguisher on the wood that was burning right above the book, hoping it wouldn't catch fire. She grabbed the book and hurriedly made her way out into the hall. She saw that the fire had now spread down to the other rooms, and that Diedre and Karl were now fighting in the waiting room.

Mina held the Grimoire in her hands and could almost feel the book make an audible sigh. "You ready?" she asked the book.

"It's about time," Jared said loudly next to her. "I thought you were going to forget about me."

She looked over her shoulder and saw Jared in head-to-toe black. "I should have abandoned you. You deserve it." He was about to say something else when a painful roar filled the air.

Mina began running toward the sound and saw that the dragon had Karl's blade embedded deep in her belly, but she had pinned him to the ground with her sheer weight. If she moved to remove the knife, Karl would escape. If she stayed where she was, slowly but surely the knife would bury itself deeper in her abdomen. The dragon roared in pain and began to bite at the Reaper's arms, making very little progress.

"Why isn't he dying?" Mina cried out.

"The Reaper is an iron giant. Her dragon claws, teeth, and fire won't be enough to kill him."

"What can kill him?" Mina wailed.

"No one knows, but she will kill herself trying to protect us," Jared said sadly. He looked upon the old dragon, and his eyes had a glassy look to them, like he was crying.

"Do it!" the dragon roared out in a high gravelly voice. Mina looked over to Diedre, whose mouth formed very distinct words. "Do it now! Use the book!" she commanded.

Karl began to panic when it heard the dragon speak and tried to fight. He bellowed and shifted shape into a man larger than an ogre but with thinner arms and legs. His skin became translucent and silver. He yelled, screamed, and punched the dragon, trying to get away. The Reaper was fearful of being imprisoned in the book.

"Why is she doing this? Tell her to stop and move away." Mina opened the book, but Jared shook his head.

"She won't. He is too strong for either of us, and we can't weaken him. If she released him, we would never catch him to entrap him in the book. It's the only way." Jared stared at the dragon regretfully and walked over to her. He touched the scales of her side, and Mina heard the dragon sigh with happiness.

"I won't do it," Mina decided, tears running down her cheeks, feeling intense loyalty to the dragon, who only moments ago she thought was the Reaper. She had assumed the dragon was trying to hurt her, but in reality, she was trying to scare her away from the hospital. Now she was protecting them.

Jared turned on her angrily. "You will. If you don't, you dishonor her death, and it will be for nothing." He continued to rub the dragon's scales, and even went so far as to touch her bleeding silver snout.

Karl reached down and grabbed a hold of the handle of the jagged knife and began to push it further into the dragon. The dragon roared out in pain. Jared tried to grab the knife from Karl, but the dragon swung her wide head and knocked Jared across the room, out of the reach of the giant.

Mina screamed as he hit the wall, but he rolled quickly to his feet and glared at her. "Do it now! Use the book and entrap them! She is dying."

"I can't!" Mina cried, tears falling freely. She crumpled to the ground and watched the dragon and giant fight. Minutes ago, she had thought Diedre was her enemy. Now she knew that wasn't true. How could she possibly entrap the dragon for eternity in a book?

Jared kneeled down next to Mina and grasped her upper arms, looking deep into her eyes. His grey eyes were red with tears. He shook her firmly but gently. "Listen to me. She is dying — she knows it. I know it. The Reaper knows it. If you don't entrap them now, then once she dies, the Reaper will be free and he will kill you."

Dark smoke filled the hallways, and she could feel heat begin to warm her back. Jared shook her again. "If you don't do it soon, we will all die anyway."

Mina looked over at Diedre and saw that her movements were slower, her bite not as aggressive, as if she was fighting just to stay on the giant. The dragon's deep blue eyes made contact with Mina's, and she saw the dragon nod in agreement.

Mina reached for the book and opened it, surprised at how many pages were now filled with trapped Fae. She found a blank page and whispered to it. The book began to glow, and light sprang forth. She turned the book toward the dragon, and the giant began to panic. He roared, kicked, clawed, and fought. The dragon watched the book expectantly, hopefully, lovingly.

The room began to spin. Chairs flew, papers ruffled, and both the dragon and giant began to slowly move toward the open pages. Diedre used her last ounce of strength to bite down hard on the iron giant as he fought against the pull of the book. A giant vortex formed out of the book, pulling them toward its pages. A chair entered the book, followed by a coffee table. The dragon and giant were much larger than a few pieces of furniture and so moved slower.

Jared threw Mina to the ground, covering her with his body as burning furniture whisked by overhead, almost hitting them. She tried to look up, but Jared kept her head buried on the ground. She could feel flames lick her feet as it passed by her and into the book. Mina and Jared began to be pulled toward the book. Loud rushing wind, howling, and screaming could be heard, until Mina realized that she was the one screaming. She had never seen the book pull this hard before, and she feared that both of them would be entrapped as well.

One moment it felt like the hospital was about to fall down on them; the next, silence. Jared waited a few seconds before moving over and letting Mina up. But he kept his arm protectively around her. Mina barely noticed. Her attention was on the damage before them; the whole wing was destroyed. The fire had been smothered by the windy vortex. A half-burned piece of paper fluttered down from the air to land on Mina's head. Pulling it off, she barely glanced at it but saw that it had Nan Taylor's name on it.

"Nan! Dr. Martin! We have to make sure they are okay." She looked to Jared, but he wasn't moving; he was staring at the book.

Reluctantly, Mina moved away from him to grab the book. She opened it up to the last page and ran her fingers across the beautiful picture of a dragon fighting a giant. "Who was she?" Mina whispered.

"A dragon," Jared answered. He touched the page tenderly, almost lovingly.

Mina touched his cheek with his hand and wiped away a stray tear. "No, who was she to you?" He wouldn't look at her.

"Probably the only one who ever really cared about me." He pressed his lips together firmly, and she could see that he was steeling himself, getting ready to hide behind his stony mask.

"That's not true." Mina pressed her forehead to Jared's, trying to comfort him. "I care."

He opened his eyes wide at her admission, and she was sucked into his beautiful grey eyes. He closed his eyes and waited with bated breath, as if savoring the moment. Reluctantly, he pulled away from her and looked at the book. "She was my nanny," Jared admitted. "She raised me since I was a kid, until I was banished. I was like a son to her.

"Why did she try to scare me?"

"I think she thought you had the Grimoire, and, like most Fae, she's not real fond of the Grimms. But I didn't even know she'd come to the human world. She must have come here shortly after I did. I was as surprised as you when she came crashing through the door."

Mina nodded silently and stood up, bringing him with her. She began to walk toward the stairway, pulling Jared behind her. Once they were on the stairs, she realized that she was still holding hands with him. She tried to draw away, but Jared held onto her hand firmly.

Not seeing any reason to let go, they walked hand in hand down the stairs. On the second floor they were met by firefighters who escorted them to safety. The parking lot was chaos, filled with fire trucks, ambulances, police, and hospital staff.

It seemed the fire had been contained to the fourth floor, and everyone had been accounted for. Everyone except nurse Diedre. Mina sat on a stretcher and was tended to by an EMT. Jared sat next to her, refusing to leave her side. It wasn't until Mina saw the tour bus and a frightened Brody and Peter waiting impatiently behind a police line that she remembered them.

She ran across the parking lot, and Brody ducked under the police tape and ran to meet her. She wasn't prepared for Brody's enthusiastic reception when he wrapped his arms around her and hugged her tightly.

"You're okay? You aren't hurt?" He looked at her and pulled her into another embrace. "I can't tell you how terrifying it was to know you were in there. And when you didn't come out with Nan, I feared the worst."

Looking up into his deep blue eyes, she could see the worry etched deep in them...and something else. She didn't have time to think, because he leaned down and kissed her. Startled, she froze for a moment before enjoying the kiss. It was soft, tender, and beautiful.

A loud clearing of the throat interrupted them. They broke apart to confront an angry Jared.

"Excuse me, but Dr. Martin is awake and asking a lot of questions. Also, they are about to transfer Nan to another hospital. I think you should get over there, if you know what I mean," Jared hinted.

Mina grabbed Peter's hand and dragged him toward the ambulance. She begged the staff to let them have a few moments with Nan before they transferred her. The EMT wasn't amused, but since Nan wasn't injured and wasn't going anywhere, he nodded.

Even in an ordinary hospital gown, Nan was beautiful. Of course, Mina knew the coma for what it truly was — an enchanted sleep. She was probably the only one who understood that Nan's glowing skin and beautiful complexion were due to Fae magic instead of medicine.

Peter stood before Nan, and he reached out to take her hand in his. He leaned down and whispered into her ear, but she didn't respond. He looked over at Mina expectantly. "So what's the plan?"

"You kiss her," Mina answered. "Just like all of the fairy tale stories where true love's kiss breaks the spell."

"Mina." Peter laughed uncomfortably. "This isn't a fairy tale. I care for her deeply, but we barely know each other. I would never, ever wish this on anyone, but I don't see how a kiss is going to wake anyone from a coma."

"It has to," Mina argued. She clenched her fists to her sides and felt doubt begin to rise up. "I know it will. She was madly in love with you, Peter. It's what all of your crazy satirical songs are about. So what are you waiting for? Kiss her. If she wakes up, you've got a great new song to write."

Brody came and stood next to Jared and watched the two argue. Finally, he chimed in. "Go ahead — I've never seen you balk at kissing a girl before," he taunted his cousin.

Sweat began to bead on Peter's forehead; he wiped it away with the sleeve of his shirt. "Well, that's because I've never kissed an almost dead girl."

"She's not dead, or almost dead. Just kiss her, and we can all go home." Mina bit her lip and jumped up and down nervously. She couldn't understand Peter's hesitation.

After much coaxing, he moved forward, placing each hand on the side of Nan's shoulders. He took a deep breath, leaned in, closed his eyes, and kissed her on her lips. A few seconds passed, and he broke the kiss.

Everyone waited with bated breath for a change. There wasn't any.

The band members sneaked under the tape and were watching the whole episode with interest. "What do you know?" Naga intoned sadly. "Beauty really is dead."

CHAPTER 25

"That can't be!" Mina was crushed. She looked at Jared, and he shrugged. She motioned to speak to him alone.

Jared nonchalantly walked over to Mina, away from the Brody and the members of the Dead Prince Society.

"What's wrong? I gave the stupid story everything it needs for the stupid fairy tale." She pushed him in the chest angrily. "I kept my part of the bargain. I found the Grimoire. I saved you. The Fates were supposed to give me a fighting chance to save her. I did that. I saved her and even brought a prince in to kiss her. You can't get a more fairy tale ending than that." Mina began pacing and twirling her hair in nervousness.

"You made a deal with the Fates?" Jared asked incredulous. "Both of them? What did they tell you?" He almost seemed panicked.

"Well, just the Queen," she answered. "But I kept my part of the bargain. She lied."

Jared thought for a moment long and hard, and studied the five boys waiting near the gurney. Four of them seemed nervous and ashamed. Only one of them seemed curious…almost thoughtful.

"Maybe you got the wrong prince." He gestured with his head toward the rest of the princes. "After all, you've got three more to choose from."

All of the doubt and insecurities vanished, and Mina looked up in hope. Of course, she had convinced all four members of the Dead Prince Society to show up at the hospital for an impromptu serenade.

"We can give it a try, but this time you have to do the convincing of kissing a girl in a coma." Mina pointed her finger at Jared and motioned to the standing boys.

"NO!" Jared reeled back in horror.

"Yes, Jared. You — you owe me." Mina stomped back to the group and waited on the side patiently. She kept looking at her watch as Jared did most of the talking. Was it only a quarter to one in the morning?

Some of the princes didn't like the idea any more than Peter did. But, after enough convincing, Constantine leaned down and gave a very quick chaste kiss. Mina kept glancing toward Dr. Martin, who was awake and having his forehead bandaged. So far, he hadn't noticed the line of boys kissing his future stepdaughter. Naga came forward, did a slight little bow, and picked up her hand. He kissed the back of her hand first. When nothing happened, he gave her a kiss on her lips.

One after another, they kissed her, and all of the kisses failed. Peter even went up and kissed her again.

"Well, that was a complete waste," Naga grumbled.

"I feel kind of weird and think we should go now," Constantine whined, and flipped his long ponytail over his shoulder. "I caught a few of the nurses looking this way, and I can see one of them talking to a police officer." He pointed, and six heads turned to look. He was right. A police officer was pointing in their direction.

"I don't know what else to do. I'm out of ideas. I was sure true love's kiss would do it." She turned her back to watch Dr. Martin come toward them. She had taken a step forward to explain when Jared grabbed her elbow, stopping her. He motioned with his head to look. Mina turned and felt her stomach drop.

Brody had moved close to Nan and was holding her hand. He was telling her how sorry he was, and how it was all his fault. Regret and guilt covered his face, but so did something else…determination. Before Mina could stop him, or tell him no, Brody squeezed Nan's hand, leaned forward, and pressed his lips to hers.

Mina's heart felt like it was in a vise being squeezed between hope and despair. She forgot to breathe as she counted the seconds of Brody and Nan's kiss. It was an eternity, or at least it felt like it. One second…two seconds…three seconds…four.

"Please!" Mina whispered, unsure whether she was saying "please, no" or "please, yes." Her eyes started to water as the familiar tingling sensation appeared, telling her Fae magic was getting involved. She turned away from Nan and Brody, unable to watch true love's kiss.

Jared looked at her strangely and then looked to Brody, and he understood. He reached for Mina and held her as a light formed around Nan and grew brighter and brighter. They could hear bells chiming. Maybe it was just the Methodist church down the road, but Mina didn't need to look to know that the kiss would work.

Nan's eyes fluttered open as Brody's kiss continued. At first she looked confused. Then she reached up with her hand to touch his face, and the kiss deepened. His breathing had become ragged and her cheeks flushed, but neither one immediately stopped the kiss.

Brody finally pulled away, his breath shaky. A small smile appeared at the corner of his mouth. Nan smiled back.

Until she noticed the night sky and her audience. Nan blushed beet red and tried to get up, but was a little weak. Brody was immediately helping her sit up.

"Why are we outside? Why do I smell smoke? Mina? Did you catch the apartment on fire?" She looked around her surroundings, at the hospital and fire trucks. "Oh, my bad, you just caught the hospital on fire," Nan joked, not knowing how close to the truth she had come.

Mina was crying. She wiped her nose on her sleeve and tried to bestow a happy smile on her face. "Hey, sleepy face. Did you have a nice nap?" Her lips quivered with hidden emotion.

Nan scrunched up her nose. "No, I had this weird dream of getting kissed by a bunch of boys." She pointed to Naga, Constantine, and Magnus. "And you were in it, and you were in it, and you were in it," she teased doing a replay of a popular scene from *The Wizard of Oz*. The smile died on her lips when she saw Peter.

Peter walked up to Nan but kept looking at his expensive black shoes. "Hey, you," he greeted her nervously.

"'Hey, you' back," Nan answered softly, not being able to meet his eyes, either. She tried to listen to Peter, but her gaze kept drifting back to Brody. They talked quietly.

Suddenly, Mina felt extremely tired. The police officer and Dr. Martin came over and weren't angry at the impromptu concert, which they credited for Nan's remarkable recovery. Dr. Martin was ecstatic and immediately called Veronica. Since they had plenty to talk about, Mina decided it was time to leave.

Her tired and sore feet had carried her across the parking lot and to the parking garage when she realized her dilemma. She had come with Brody to the hospital, but she didn't have the strength or courage to get a ride home with him. Not after witnessing their magical and awakening kiss. Collapsing on a cement parking bumper, Mina rested her head in her hands.

She pulled out the black leather book and opened it to its newest page. It was a picture of Nan sleeping on the gurney while Brody, the four band members, Jared, Mina, and Dr. Martin gathered around her outside a glass hospital. Mina felt her lips pull up into a wry smile. When she counted the heads out loud, she came to seven, plus a prince. She was even more surprised when she turned the page and saw another picture of Brody and Nan kissing, proving that she had completed Sleeping Beauty's story as well.

Her skin started to tingle, and a shiver of power ran up her spine. The smell of gardenias encompassed Mina, a sure sign that a Fae was opening a gate. Mina had a feeling she knew which one was coming over. A flash of light appeared and quickly dissipated. Mina refused to look. The smell of gardenias permeated the area.

"Two birds with one story," Mina said out loud to no one in particular. "It could have been a disaster if it weren't for Diedre's sacrifice."

A woman's voice spoke out of the darkness. "Yes, it could have been, but sometimes one must sacrifice a pawn."

Mina turned toward the sound, but she was too exhausted to stand or give the Queen a curtsey. Maeve came and stood before Mina, and raised her eyebrow at Mina's lack of respect. Her dress was a beautiful dark blue with gold macramé overlay.

"I see you have kept your part of the bargain and reclaimed the Grimoire once again," Maeve's voice had a distinct royal undertone in it.

Mina found herself snorting in disdain. "No thanks to you. In fact, I was of half a mind to ignore our bargain and leave the Grimoire in the room to burn. It would have saved us all a whole lot of trouble. Your kind wouldn't be trapped anymore — I wouldn't have to finish the stupid quests — "

"Don't even joke about such things. You have no idea of the power of the Grimoire." She stepped forward, and her voice rose in pitch but her face stayed impassive.

Fed up, Mina stood to confront the Queen, her anger spilling out in waves. "Don't play me. I'm not dumb. He's your son!" Mina yelled.

Maeve stopped moving. Only the tremor in her voice gave her away. "I have no idea what you mean."

"Jared. He's your son. And he is somehow bound to the Grimoire. It can't hurt him or capture him because he is inexplicably linked to it." Mina began pacing back and forth, her hands waving in the air, and the picture became crystal clear.

Maeve stood frozen and her chin rose high in the air, neither denying the claims nor agreeing.

"I started to piece it together when Ever said pixies don't get along with ogres. If anyone knew Jared, it was Ever. It's when I figured out he had to have royal blood in him. Only the Royals can transform to multiple shapes."

Mina threw her head back and laughed. "I get it. He's like a genie in a bottle, and that's his prison. I can only see and talk to him when I'm in possession of the book. It's why he disappeared the same time the Grimoire did. It's why you wanted me to get the book back so badly. It had nothing to do with the innocent Fae being trapped inside. The Reapers work for you. They kill the Grimms whenever we come close to finishing the quest. But this one didn't want to listen to you. You couldn't control this Reaper. It's because you wanted your son back safe and sound. But at the expense of what? Nan, Dr. Martin, me, and Diedre?"

The Queen's face blanched, and she looked pained. Mina thought it was something she'd said until she saw the Queen reach out past her to someone standing behind her. Mina turned to see Jared, unmoving. He was livid. He moved forward, toward his mother. Mina backed up, thinking he would go and take sides with the Queen. Instead, he came and stood directly in front of Mina, as if he were protecting her from his own mother.

"Hello, Mother." Jared's voice dripped acid.

"Why, Jared," she soothed, "you are looking well." Her hand nervously went to her hair to pat it in place.

He ignored her. "Did Dad tell the Reaper to go after Mina?"

Maeve paled again. "No, that was an accident how he stumbled upon her. You were there — you knocked the tree down to save her from the car."

"I know that. But was it you or Dad who told the Reaper to kill an innocent girl, knowing that I would tell Mina and she would walk into your trap." Jared's fists shook, and Mina could hear his knuckles cracking.

"Don't you raise your voice to me, young man. It was your insolence that got you banished and put you in your present circumstance. It wasn't me, but can you blame your father for trying to kill the Grimm and get the book back safely?"

"So, what? I can be trapped in limbo for years on end, waiting for the next Grimm? I've had it. I'm tired of being your pawn. I'm tired of you and my brother manipulating Mina for your own enjoyment. It's sick!"

Mina stood back and waited, stunned. This was the first time she had heard Jared ever mention a brother.

"Teague can get a little carried away, but I'm sure you know the reasons. He is your brother and is just as tired of his constraints as you are of yours." Maeve could see that she wasn't winning any popularity points by bringing up her other son.

"Rein him in," Jared argued back.

She tried a different approach. "I was only trying to do what was best for you, and I don't think that this girl is what's

best for you. I can see you are becoming attached, and that's
— "

"Leave," Jared interrupted her. "You've done enough
damage here already. Just leave."

The Queen's pride wouldn't let her leave without a last
word. "Don't think you can save this one. I told you not to get
attached. After all, they all die in the end."

Frustrated at being talked about as if she weren't there,
Mina finally pushed Jared to the side. "I've fulfilled my end of
the bargain. Although I think you owe me for saving your
son."

Maeve's hair began to blow from her power. "I don't owe
you anything," she retorted.

"That remains to be seen." Mina raised her chin in
challenge.

The Queen waved her hand. A bright blaring gateway
appeared, and she stepped through. The parking garage was
once again dark except for the streetlight and the few
emergency lights. Jared watched his mother leave and stared at
the empty space where the door had been before turning to
Mina with a sad smile on his face.

She began to walk away, thinking maybe she could get a
ride home from the police. But then she would have to explain
to her mother what happened. Mina inwardly cringed.

"Hey, wait up!" Jared called after her. Since he wasn't
trying to hide anything from her anymore, he used a bit of
magic and made a car appear next to him.

Mina turned to stare at a bright red Mustang with Jared
smiling broadly at the wheel.

"It's a little flashy," Mina commented wryly.

Jared shrugged, and the car shifted into a Toyota Prius.
Mina looked from the parking garage to the ambulance to see
Brody standing very close to Nan. He held her hand, and they

both looked shaken, unsure, and scared. Mina squeezed her eyes to keep the tears from falling. She looked up, took a deep breath, and let Jared drive her home.

CHAPTER 26

Life returned to normal, or almost normal. Nan was back at school a few days later, fully recovered and the belle of Kennedy High School. Nan chattered a mile a minute and picked up life right where she'd left off. She was back to texting on her phone, taking hundreds of pictures, and even making snide remarks about Savannah and Pri. But there were a few minor details that had changed. Nan was no longer obsessed with the band the Dead Prince Society. In fact, she had gotten rid of all of her posters, T-shirts, and CDs.

Mina had tried to bring up what had happened, but her best friend simply refused to talk about it. She wasn't sure, but Mina thought the breakup was due to the fact that Brody was the one to wake Nan up from the coma. She didn't think Peter could handle the idea of being in competition with his cousin over a girl.

The other big change was the addition to their lunch table seating. Their lunch duo turned into a quintet, with the addition of a turbulent pixie, a mischievous Jared, and a very subdued Brody.

She should have been thrilled to have her crush and almost boyfriend sitting at the same table with her every day at lunch, but instead it was torture. Brody sat across from Mina and spent most of the time listening intently and observing Nan's every move. If she tripped, he immediately grabbed her elbow and kept her safe. He refused to let her carry her own lunch tray or book bag. He hovered over Nan, not in a suffocating kind of way, but in a knight in shining armor way.

Mina's fork shook as she picked up a piece of French fry from her tray and tried to stomach eating the bland flash-fried food. Everything she ate tasted like ash. Maybe it was her jealousy gnawing away in the pit of her stomach again. She tried to take a deep breath and think positively and not be jealous, because that was what had gotten her in trouble in the first place.

Nan wasn't sure what to make of the attention. She at first tried to ignore Brody, but after a while she caved in to his charms and good looks. After all, if Nan was the fairest in the school, it seemed only right that the school's prince was her boyfriend. Every once in a while Mina would look up and catch Brody staring at her in confusion and sadness, as if he too knew what they had and lost. They were both haunted by the lingering emotions from that one kiss.

Mina sighed heavily and looked back down at her plate. Ever made a comment about how the food was the best she had ever tasted. When Mina didn't respond, she reached over and grabbed a fry off Mina's unguarded plate. Ever was the oddest addition to their table. Most of the time, she would be sullen and moody. Other times, she tried to take advantage of Mina's incoherent situation, like stealing French fries. But it was obvious she was happy that Mina had gotten Jared back. What their actual relationship status was Mina didn't really know, and it seemed like neither Jared nor Ever wanted to elaborate.

Jared smiled more, as if a giant weight — or more likely secrets — had been lifted from his shoulders. He seemed happy, content that the Grimoire was back with Mina, but what that really entailed, she wasn't sure. She had been reluctant to question his duties as the servant of the Grimoire.

He took a bite out of his burger and smiled at Mina. She felt her heart speed up a little bit, and her cheeks reddened when she remembered how he had held her hand and comforted her. Ever saw the interlude and interrupted the moment by telling a joke. Mina looked over and saw Brody watching her again, and she felt her stomach drop. She couldn't do this anymore. She picked up her tray, disposed of the food in the garbage, and left the school cafeteria, leaving Jared behind. She reached into her jacket pocket and touched the leather-bound Grimoire, and felt it grow warm at her touch. Mina knew that she was never fully alone.

It wasn't until later that night, when she sat alone atop her roof on her lawn chair, that she was finally able to rest and think about last week's events. She had found another small gnome statue at the thrift store and had decided to add it to her growing collection. She thought Sir Nomer needed company, especially of the female variety. She set the girl gnome statue, which she had named Princess Nomita, next to Sir Nomer. She couldn't help but laugh at their jovial positions.

"What a trivial pastime," a male voice taunted her.

Mina's lips turned up slyly as she spun around with a quick comeback, ready to assault Jared with a nasty remark. Except that it wasn't Jared who walked around, studying her retreat.

He was remarkably handsome like Jared, and similar in many ways. He was tall and slender, and his hair had a slightly lighter tone. He wore all black. But his clothes looked like they were centuries out of date. When he turned to look Mina square in the face, she knew it couldn't be Jared.

The person standing in front of her wearing a self-righteous smirk had dark blue eyes, while Jared's were a stormy grey. Immediately, Mina knew who she was dealing with, and her temper began to rise in barely controlled hatred.

"What, no hello?" He smiled smugly, raising his hands in a welcoming manner.

"You're not welcome here," Mina told him.

"Ah, so I take it you know who I am." His blue eyes became darker, and his smile fell from his lips.

"Yes, you must be Teague." Mina's words were clipped and controlled. "You're the one to blame for everything." She slowly reached toward her pocket of her jacket and the Grimoire. Teague saw her deliberate movement and grabbed her wrist painfully.

"Ah! Let's leave my little brother out of this for the moment. What I have to say is between you and me." She glared at him in defiance, refusing to flinch from the pain. He smiled at her strength and then released his grip on her wrist. "So you overheard my mother call me Teague, but do you know I am also called by a different name?" he taunted.

Her lips curled up in a knowing smile. "I know. I looked it up at the library. Teague has many meanings, but the most common is Storyteller or, in your case, Story." She watched as Teague's eyebrows rose in surprise. She had caught him off guard.

"Very good. I'm impressed. It seems I may have underestimated you. You are the very first Grimm ever to figure out our secret." He raised his hand slowly and brushed his knuckles down the side of Mina's cheek. Her skin crawled from the contact.

He chuckled. "So, do you like my parting gift? I thought it would be nice to give you what you wanted for once. You had been so miserable the last few weeks when I erased your friends' memories. I was tired of watching you mope around, all pathetic. I thought you would like this ending better. Your best friend and boyfriend get to live happily ever after." He was extremely pleased with himself and smiled widely.

Bile rose up in Mina's throat at Teague's obvious machinations to try to break her and to use her friends for his games.

"It's fine," Mina taunted back. Stepping forward, she pushed into Teague's chest. He moved back a few steps. "I, too, know how to play this game, and I'm getting better at it." She began to chuckle, and the smile dropped from Teague's handsome face.

"What?" he asked worriedly. "What is so funny?"

"Nothing," she answered coyly. "It's just so much easier knowing that it is you that I have to overcome, not some magical book that exists in the Fae world. Because if your situation is similar to Jared's, and I believe it is, then your existence is bound to a book as well. So, in other words, if you die, I kill the Story, which means, bye-bye quests, and bye-bye curse." Mina walked over to the rooftop and grabbed a spade she used to transfer her potted plant.

All of the color drained from Teague's face as Mina spelled out his secret. She kept adjusting the handle of the spade in her hand, testing its weight.

"You wouldn't dare!" he joked nervously. "The Fates would send more Reapers after you. In fact, all of the Fae would try to kill you." He backed up and tripped backward over Mina's lawn chair, breaking it. Teague fumbled with the plastic furniture and finally freed himself from it.

"Tell me something new. They've been manipulating our original bargain and hunting my family down for hundreds of years. But nobody has ever tried to bring the fight to them. That's all going to change, starting now." She had advanced upon Teague and swiped at his midriff with the spade. He jumped back and fled to the other side of the roof. "This Grimm will no longer follow the rules."

"You don't know what you would be doing. You would be declaring war!" He looked scared, but not because of Mina's spade. He was scared by what she was proposing.

"Then prepare for war, Story." Mina took the spade and began to drag it across the roof, scratching out a very definite line in the cement. "The lines of battle have been drawn. Tell your King and Queen to send their best, because *this* tale is about to be rewritten."

End of Book 2

Chanda Hahn takes her experience as a children's pastor, children's librarian and bookseller to write compelling and popular fiction for teens.

She was born in Seattle, Washington, grew up in Nebraska, and currently resides in Portland, Oregon with her husband and their twin children; Aiden and Ashley.

Visit Chanda Hahn's website to learn more about her other forthcoming books. **www.chandahahn.com**

Also by Chanda Hahn

Unfortunate Fairy Tale Series
UnEnchanted
Fairest
Fable

The Iron Butterfly
The Steele Wolf
The Silver Siren

Acknowledgements

I want to say a special thanks to everyone who helped me with this book. Whether it was inspiring words, encouragement, editing or watching my twins so I can write. Thank you: Alison Brace, Ann-Marie Morgan, Stacey Wallace Benefiel, Mandy Pratt and my husband Philip Hahn.